AN MMF MILITARY ROMANCE

# PREYLESS

## C. S. SILVERNE

Second Edition: March 2026

Copy and Line Editing by Sadie, Dot The i Edit

Cover Artwork: Valerie

Interior Formatting: Disturbed Valkyrie Designs (@disturbedvalkyriedesigns)

ISBN: 978-1-972811-02-3

www.cssilverneauthor.com

# PLAYLIST

Face Down — The Red Jumpsuit App
Slow Down — Chase Atlantic
My Happy Ending — Avril Lavigne
The Great Escape — BOYS LIKE GIRLS
If It Means A Lot To You — A Day To Remember
Silence — Marshmello, Khalid
Provider — Sleep Token
V. A. N. — Bad Omens, Poppy
I'm With You — Avril Lavigne
All I Want — A Day To Remember
Animals — Maroon 5
Good For You — Selena Gomez, A$AP Rocky
Decode — Paramore
Human — Rag'n'Bone Man
Dandelions - slowed + reverb — Ruth B.
Way Down We Go — KALEO

Chlorine — Twenty One Pilots
My Happy Ending — Avril Lavigne
Undeniable — Kygo (feat. X Ambassadors)
Stargazing — Myles Smith

**Listen to the full playlist here <3**

*Preyless* contains content that may be sensitive to some.
*Please protect yourself and your mental health.*

References to anxiety, child abuse (past, mentioned briefly), C-PTSD, the death of a spouse via drinking and driving (past), domestic abuse (past, not between current main characters), emotional and psychological abuse (past, not between current main characters), light stalking, manipulation, mentions of potential infertility, military main characters, miscarriage (past, mentioned), obsession, pregnancy, trauma flashbacks, and victim blaming.

Sexual content includes aftercare, baby fever, blood play, blowjobs, breeding kink, choking, daddy kink, deep-throating, dom/sub relationships, dominance, explicit sex scenes, fear play, threesomes, knife play, light degradation, mask play, masturbation, praise kink, primal play, the use/mention of safe-words, sex without a condom, sexting, spanking, and whiskey spitting (intoxication play).

# RESOURCES

*Preyless* touches on themes of domestic abuse and the pain of being blamed after a miscarriage. While this story is fictional and focuses on healing through kink, I know these experiences are very real—and that so many people live through them every single day.

With the help of others, I've included links below to charities, organizations, and other resources that might offer support. Taking that first step to leave a harmful situation is unbelievably hard, but please know this: needing help doesn't make you weak. It means you're human—and incredibly strong for choosing to keep going. You're a total badass for that, in fact.

XO,


C. S. Silverne

Adalyn Rose Foundation
National Coalition Against Domestic Violence
RAINN
Return to Zero: H. O. P. E
Safe Horizon
The Joyful Heart Foundation
The National Domestic Violence Hotline
The Tears Foundation

*To anyone who has endured abuse of any kind.*

*There are many different definitions of "love" in our world —but that is not one of them.*

*I hope you're safe now. And even more than that—I hope you find happiness and peace soon, if you haven't yet. You deserve nothing but healing, patience, and **genuine** love.*

# PROLOGUE

I'VE ALWAYS WONDERED what it would feel like to die.

Well, in a way.

I never *exactly* wondered what it would feel like regarding the action itself, nor had I ever planned a death of any kind—for myself or others. Death, for the most part, was painful in nearly all ways of its delivery; regardless of how some felt about it. And if you just so happened to die in a way that didn't stem from the agony of pain or sickness...then you probably were lucky enough to only spread that pain onto the souls of others.

Nevertheless, death was painful.

Or it should have been.

Right?

A sick part of me hoped it was for the ones who hurt others freely.

Who damaged them.

Who made them crave things people shouldn't generally crave.

But over the last three months, I had come to an agonizing, yet truthful understanding.

I would never know.

Pain was nothing new to me, but I didn't like thinking about it until I had to. In utter honesty, nothing good ever came of it. I was exhausted from living in my past relationship—that may as well have been a spider's web effect—when I finally had a chance for growth in the future.

So, instead, I pictured my own version of Rapunzel.

Locked in a tower, desolate and alone, until a version of Prince Charming came for me.

A Prince Charming who had come to rescue me, after all.

Someone who would grow to love me. Who would show me that I wouldn't and shouldn't have to feel *his* wrath or disappointment breathing down my neck anymore. That I wouldn't have to provide for someone who had lost themselves in the hope of our ruin.

A Prince Charming who would simply love me like I craved.

Like I deserved.

But my life was no fairytale, and regardless of how much I wished to escape it and be reincarnated into the next one—preferably as a peaceful frog on a lily pad with no worries outside of what bug I would eat that day—I was fucked.

So, instead, I thought about death. About how

sweetly relieving it must feel to finally give into the confinements and release of life.

No more shitty job.

No more shitty life.

There was only peace.

I should've avoided that train of thought, though.

Anger only clawed its way up my throat every time my mind drifted in its direction.

Because he was dead, and while I only hoped he was in hell, I was left alive to suffer through the trauma and aftermath of him. Of having to heal from his hands, words, actions, and toxicity after the unimaginable.

If only...

"Alright, do you have any questions for me before you start?" The man in front of me asked, raising his bushy gray eyebrows expectantly. The question forced me out of my thoughts, and I looked at him, trying to appear as though I wasn't thinking about *death* for the last ten minutes of my *technical* orientation.

As all girls do, or something.

The new job just so happened to be working night shifts in a random hotel, in a city that I've only lived in for a solid seventy-two hours, that *also* happened to be two streets away from a central naval base.

My last-ditch attempt to escape the hellhole that was my life.

I definitely had a death wish.

"No, sir," I replied, smiling politely. A blush started to mar my pale complexion under the intensity of his stare. Men intimidated me beyond belief, and while I had the faux-confidence complexion of any SEAL around here, I couldn't stop the ringing in my ears or the panic in my veins.

One one-thousand, two one-thousand, three one-thousand...

Safe, I reminded myself. You're safe now.

He sighed, and those bushy eyebrows of his lowered skeptically. He looked as tired as my soul felt, and I honestly felt bad for the man. "And you're sure you don't mind staying on the premises? I know we're a bit remote compared to the main parts of Norfolk and Virginia Beach, but I could really use the help running this joint. Driving out here every day is exhausting."

I forced a chuckle out of my sore throat.

The throat that carried stark, black and blue hand prints underneath my black turtleneck.

Even stopping at the local convenience store for a cheap, knock-off brand of color correcting concealer did little to hide the bruises. Or the cut that graced the left side of my temple.

Hubby-dearest was just too drunk to realize he had gone too far, leaving bruises where everyone could see them this time.

Before he climbed into his car and—

Forcing myself to blink the thoughts away, I hid the wince from my chuckle and smiled politely. "It's truly no burden to me. I think I'm at a point in my life where nature, remote locations, and keeping my head down sound perfect."

He squinted at me, and my heart dropped the slightest bit.

I needed this job because I needed somewhere to

sleep—let alone somewhere to figure out what I was doing with my life next—and I would be damned if I ever touched the life insurance money that *he* left me with.

It would be split and donated to the local domestic violence shelters by the end of the week.

At least he would do something good in his last moments. Even if it still made me want to fly back to Oregon and spit on his grave.

Regardless, I needed the man in front of me to give me a chance.

He shook his head before continuing. "Well, if you say so, kid. When I was twenty-two, I certainly preferred to travel and drink, but I know jack-shit about this generation. Maybe there is some hope for you lot, after all. As long as you're a good worker, I believe we will get along just fine."

I giggled, though cursed internally at the painful wince that immediately wracked my features. Thankfully, he had turned his back away from me, and I was able to school my features back to normal moments later when he returned his heavy gaze back on me. "And you're comfortable with the dress code?"

"Business casual, right?"

He nodded. "That's right. I'm good with jeans—hell, you can even wear sweatshirts and comfortable tops. I know how drafty it can get here sometimes. I just ask that you don't show up to work in pajamas. Or...nothing at all, like Larry once did. I still have to scrub that surveillance footage from my brain after showing it to the police."

My mouth parted in shock. "Larry?"

"Bath salts," was all he said, and I had to force myself not to burst out laughing.

Even managing to not tip up my lips in humor was a challenge.

Laughing in front of your elderly boss regarding the mention of hardcore drugs, though...probably wouldn't have been the best of ideas.

I just hoped Larry wouldn't be paying me a visit during one of my night shifts.

I was tiny, malnourished, and exhausted. Living in my car until I could make it to this interview was hard enough, and I certainly did not need to deal with him, too.

Nevertheless, his lore sounded hilarious.

He tapped the cold black metal desk that separated us with his knuckles before standing and grabbing his coat. "Well, you have my number if you need me. I know you said you could start immediately, and there's truly not much else you can do except hand people their keys and keep surveillance for the morning shift, so I will leave you to it."

I stood with him, rubbing the sweat off my hands onto my denim jeans before extending a palm out to him to shake. "Yes, sir. I'll text you with any questions I have, too."

On a cracked phone that had...zero minutes on it.

I'd need to correct that as soon as possible.

At least the hotel had full access to Wi-Fi.

He nodded again, shaking my hand politely before passing me with a smile. "Welcome to the Wooded Lodge, Rory. And call me John, would you? I'm old, and probably old fashioned, but the 'sir' still makes me feel like I'm one breath away from a cane."

I nodded with him, a hint of a smile on my face. I watched out the windows as he left the building and began making the trek to his own car. The sun had begun to set, filling the sky with streaks of oranges and pinks—even hidden behind so many of the favored trees near the forest trails by the beach—and I felt a semblance of peace gnawing at my insides for the first time in months.

A semblance of warmth, even.

A breath of relief flew out of me at the feeling and realization.

I got the job.

I escaped my husb—*ex*-husband.

I had a place to live...even if it technically *was* my job.

Everything was going to look up from here.

It was finally time for me to heal.

One way or another.

## ONE YEAR LATER

"HONEY, I'M HOME!" I singsonged out as I entered the foyer of our town home and hung my keys on the hooks by the door next to Casey's, showing he was here, too. I smiled appreciatively at the sight, and even more so at the dirty thoughts that immediately followed. Exhaustion marred every inch of my existence after the workday, and yet, all I wanted to do was bury my cock in my boyfriend until he was putty in my hands before forcing him to milk the frustration out of me, stroke by stroke.

I grunted at the thought.

Fuck.

The thought alone had me growing stiff in my uniform.

I was nothing if not obsessed with the man down the hall.

He was my everything. I'd marry him tomorrow if I could.

To fully claim him. To *own* him.

The thought gave me pause as I began to unlace my work boots, as it often did.

I sighed tiredly. God, did I ever want to call Casey my *husband*.

But for years, there had been one thing holding me back. And while it probably didn't make sense in the heads of others—it was more than vital to me, to the dynamic of us and how we would last with such a unique need.

A family.

A woman.

A woman, just for us.

While we were exponentially happy together, there was always something missing between us. We had realized years ago that it wasn't only a feminine touch, but also...the future that a woman could bring.

We needed a third.

And that certainly threw a wrench into the aspect of marriage when any and all attempts in finding a third, let alone a third who could deal with our fucked up natures and possessive qualities, may not even want an ownership as intense as we craved it.

Granted, even in the modern day and age, marrying in polyamorous relationships was a complete and utter bitch.

But it didn't matter.

If you were mine, then you were mine. And that meant you were also *ours.*

Casey's sarcastic voice filled the end of the hall, and I smiled as the longing thoughts quickly left my head at the sound of his voice. "My darling boyfriend is back from war. Whatever shall I do to dote on him?"

"You know it was just a twelve-hour shift, right?"

He met me with a blank stare. "Do you want your dick sucked or not?"

A laugh bellowed out of me. "Oh? You sure dropped that old-timey tone real quick. What bold words."

He shrugged before crossing his arms and leaning against the doorway as I continued unlacing my boots —and I could have sworn that my mouth salivated as I stared at the man before me. His blond hair was wet and wild, likely from coming straight out of the shower, and his sharp jawline sported the beginning of a short beard. He was in comfortable clothing—meager shorts and a black T-shirt—and yet, I had to fight the urge to not go over there and bite one of his tattooed biceps.

His voice cut me out of my thoughts again, and my brown eyes snapped to his blue ones. "You alright over there, Wolfe? You look like you're hungry. You don't need me to undo those laces, do you? I know I bottom a lot in this relationship, but that"—he pointed to my boots that were *still* untied—"is just pitiful, ya know?"

My voice was rough. "You know what it does to me when you refer to me by my call sign."

"I do."

"Are you trying to get fucked within an inch of your

life, Wraithe? Because you're getting really close to achieving that, if that's what you're looking for."

His lips lifted in a smirk. "Maybe I am."

A pairing smile slid across my face as I finally slid the leather boots off of my feet and pushed them to the side. Looking directly at Casey, I pointed to him, and then to the floor in front of me with a snap of my fingers. "Kneel, pretty boy."

My chest thrummed with pride as I watched him stalk toward me and drop to his knees, right where I told him to do so. *What a good boy.* Power dynamics in BDSM were always so judged, and I'd never get over the oddness when the simplest of actions such as kneeling made me ecstatic. "Mmm. Such a respected, scary SEAL during the day. And yet, just my good boy when we're home. Isn't that right?"

Casey stared directly in my eyes without hesitation before he responded, "You're an asshole. You know that, right?"

I smirked. He could say all he wanted, but we both knew he loved it as much as I did. "Yup."

"Why do I even put up with you?"

I smiled. "Because you're utterly in love with me. And I happen to be attractive *and* hung, which should be considered bonus points of some kind."

"Oh, is that so? *Daddy?* Have you ever heard of an ego check? You might need one."

I scoffed as one of my eyebrows lifted in question. The hand that was resting on my thigh moved to wrap around his throat gently, and I smirked once more as I felt his Adam's apple swallow roughly against my palm. I hadn't even begun pressing against his pressure points yet. "I don't hear you complaining much when I'm bottomed out inside that pretty ass of yours."

"I don't think you hear much when you're bottomed out in me. You're ruthless when you're horny, but also have a one-track mind."

The *brat.*

I squeezed his pressure points and took the utmost satisfaction in the pretty shade of red he turned. "You wanna repeat that, pretty boy?"

"No, Sir," he managed to get out, although I saw something twinkle in his eye.

Pleasure satiated every part of me as I watched his eyes close in submission, and I knew then and there that he would let me do absolutely anything I wanted to him.

Granted, I had already known that. But I still loved the reminder.

Too bad he was in fucking trouble for being a brat.

I could make him suffer a little bit; a little teasing never hurt.

My cock stirred behind my uniform once again at the thought, and I raised my other hand to cup his cheek fondly. My fingers danced across his pouty lips as I spoke. "I should fuck this bratty mouth of yours, you know. It was a long day. You're mine, after all. I may adore you with everything I am, but you're still my stress relief toy. You'd love that though, wouldn't you? Being a toy for Daddy."

My hand relinquished its squeeze enough to let him speak. "So much," he groaned.

"Cup me through my uniform then. Go on," I goaded him.

Fire licked up my spine as he did so without question, and I bit back a groan deep in my throat as he squeezed his hand.

And just like that—I was hard as a rock.

My hand squeezed at his throat again. Not hard enough to constrict his air, but enough so to show my possessiveness. "I never said you could play with it," I warned.

"You never said I could masturbate earlier, either, but I did that. And guess what, the world didn't explode." He made a mocking, gasping face. "Would you look at that? I don't always have to follow the rules, it seems."

My mouth dropped. Two strikes in one day, and we hadn't even covered the first, completely out-of-pocket fuck up. "You came without me knowing?"

"Yep."

"Mmm. Okay," I started, swallowing roughly as he squeezed my hard length again. He was trying to break my stubborn guard, and any other day, it probably would have worked.

Not that day, though.

I took a deep breath. I was a trained sailor *and* special operations agent.

He would *not* win.

My voice came out rough. "How was your day?"

He snorted. "You're asking me about my day? Really? When I'm like this?"

"Yes."

"It was good. Thank you, Daddy. How was your day?"

"Just wonderful," I let out sarcastically, groaning as his hand shifted up my length. "Certainly no complaints. Other than, ya know, work—and an odd email I got."

"An odd email?"

"Mhhmm," I ground out as he stroked me over my uniform more. I wouldn't have been surprised if precum was dripping from the head of my cock already. I needed to get out of these camo pants, and fast.

"You sound needy and dumb, Wolfe. Maybe you need to use your boy. Yeah?"

Oh, the pleasure that marred me as I smirked down at him.

He asked the perfect question.

With a finality in my tone, I leaned down and whispered directly in his ear, "I would, but my boy broke his rules today, so I'm going to go jerk off in the shower. Where you can only watch from outside the glass doors, and that's *if* they don't fog up too fast. How's that for your *good day*?"

His mouth dropped open as I stood, laughing and walking toward the main bathroom.

With an unbelievably aching cock.

Having your own dick completely belong to someone else was humbling in times like that.

"That's rude!" he called at my back.

I turned my head back enough to respond. "So is signing us up for a kink app using my *work* email address, thinking I wouldn't find out, and then masturbating without my knowledge. Enjoy your punishment, pretty boy. We'll talk about this when I'm clean and sated."

"WOULD YOU QUIT POUTING?" Aiden murmured against my neck as I forced myself *not* to enjoy the bliss that was his heat or stubble rubbing against my skin. I wasn't even *actually* upset, but I had a bratty persona to follow through on, so therefore, the scowl on my face stayed put. "It was a three minute shower. There's literally no way I could have washed my ass, let alone the rest of me, *and* finished in that time frame. I'm not eighteen anymore. I can't just come from the wind."

One of my eyebrows perked up.

He did have a point there.

I grumbled as I snuggled impossibly closer to him, even though it was *his* entire weight on top of me, rather than the other way around. "You know you're only thirty-six, right? You act like you have the penis of a seventy-year-old some days. And even then, some of those old men could get it."

Slowly, he picked his head up to look at me, and I chortled at the expression on his face. "Sometimes, I truly forget who has the most daddy issues until you say stupid shit like that."

"What? Take some testosterone and an ED pill. Right as rain. I'd fuck one."

"We are not inviting a seventy-year-old man into this house," he deadpanned.

"Oh, c'mon. It could be fun! You don't want to feel a wrinkly ballsack? Maybe even call him grandpa? Talk about a power dynamic, for sure."

I groaned as his head smacked down on my chest. *Hard.* "No. Hardest of passes. It would just remind me of raisins, and I would rather croak before he could at that point."

"That's just disrespectful to grandpa," I chided.

"Casey," he groaned out slowly, shaking his head. I chuckled as I ran a hand down his back comfortingly. His muscles were tense—his posture always on guard, even when he didn't have to be. Almost like he was prepared for a masked gunman to walk through the door at any given point.

Granted, with our career, it wouldn't be too far of a stretch.

I was more than positive there were hits on us from other countries at that point.

It didn't matter, though.

We were contracted to the government to act as the boogeymen.

And while we were more skilled in hunting and

tracking than the final blow, nothing could scare what has already been scared to death and back.

Aiden's voice cut through my thoughts. "I can literally feel you thinking your brain away. It's already made its way to the Midwest. It's running as fast as *Forest Gump.*"

"Yeahhhh," I droned out as my hand continued rubbing the tension away from his back. "It's been one of those kinds of days."

"I thought you said you had a good day?"

"I did. You know how I get, though. That last mission fucked with me. It always gives me some more perspective."

His response was dryer than the desert. "Any more perspective and I'm gonna have to start calling you Gandalf."

"Now look who's bringing up old men."

Once again, his head lifted, and our eyes collided. Though, that time, his gaze was laced with concern as he stared directly into my soul. The man knew me better than I knew myself, and it was as endearing as it was utterly annoying.

"I'm okay. I promise. They just..." I scrubbed at my face tiredly. "There were kids. You saw them. You'd think it would get easier—the missions, the shit we see—but when they go after innocent children, it hits harder."

"I know, baby."

"How do you manage it so well?" I asked.

It was the one thing I always admired about the man above me.

His call name was Wolfe in the field because he was

an elite tracker and hunter. But after knowing him for so long, I thought it fit his strength more than his skill.

Always the leader.

Even when he saw the horrors of his own men firsthand.

He shrugged. "Nothing can hurt me as much as my dad used to. Not only did he hurt me, but he hurt Rosie and Caleb, too. And I had to watch it all. I grew up knowing that evil existed in this world far before I got into international affairs, pretty boy."

I knew his answer.

I knew him.

That didn't stop my heart from panging, though.

Aiden continued as he laid back down on me. *Who would have known that the six-four, muscular giant was such a snuggler?* "Let's get off this subject. How about instead you tell me why the hell you signed us up for a kink app—of all apps—on a *work* email address? I'm not letting that one go, Wraithe. You're lucky I unsubscribed from the marketing and update shit as soon as I saw it."

That question made my face scrunch up sheepishly.

Okay, so it *was* a very bad decision on my part. I could have used any other email address. Using a government one was definitely out of pocket.

But..."It got your attention, did it not?"

He grunted. "Obviously."

Picking my head up, I wiggled away enough to grab my phone off the nightstand. Nearly impossible due to the two-hundred-something-pound man on top of me, but I persevered. Once it was in my hand, I quickly unlocked the phone, opened the app, and handed it to him. "It's called *Preyless*. I found it on a random forum."

"I saw that much. Why do we have it? And on the *work email?*"

I groaned. "I'm getting there!"

"Speed it up, grandpa-lover."

My eyes rolled petulantly. I already knew he was never going to let that one go. "Well, we've been talking about adding in a third for months now, yeah? And obviously, all of the dating apps are an absolutely horrendous way to go. You're too *grrrrr, ima eat you*, and I'm too *play with my hair for the rest of eternity*. No girl is going to want us there. In fact, with us being military men on top of that—they will probably call the police on us."

"...Okay," he said with his face pinched as he started scrolling through the app.

I had to swallow my laugh.

Oh, how I found myself hilarious. Even if he didn't.

We already knew that unless you were a barrack bunny, you probably didn't *actually* like military men. The abusive assholes gave all of us a shitty reputation.

But...if you happened to like certain kinks...it worked out.

I continued. "So, I present to you, *Preyless*. An app dedicated to the darker side of kinks, or so it's advertised. Similar to that one BDSM website we were on once upon a time. But...less forum-y. There's not as many help columns or things on this one. It's actually meant to connect you with others who know what they want."

"Alright. So, you're hoping that we find our dream girl on a *fetish* app. I gotta hand it to you—that is a new one. And here I thought you couldn't surprise me anymore after six years."

I smiled cheesily. "Well, even if we did join Finder, they would run for the hills the second they found out that you wanted to chase them through the woods and breed them in the mud."

He scoffed, indignant. "You don't know that!"

"I guarantee you that they would point out the logistics of fucking in mud and how it would probably give them a UTI."

"We have a doctor on base. It's fine," he grumbled again. "Okay, whatever. So, let's say that all of the cards fall in order, *somehow*, and we find our dream girl. What then? We're not looking for a threesome—we're looking for a *third*. Nothing less. Shouldn't we try some polyamorous websites or something first?"

I raised one of my arms and laid it behind my head. I watched with humor and cockiness as his eyes drifted away from my phone to my arms, and I had the sneaking suspicion that he was going to bite the shit out of me soon. I started again before he could have the chance to bruise me. "I thought about that. Until I started scrolling...and I found someone."

His eyes snapped to mine in shock, biceps forgotten. "What?! You found someone? Already?"

"I did. I haven't messaged her yet, obviously. I wasn't going to do anything without your approval—"

"—Except masturbate."

"Oh, get over it! I didn't even do it. I was just trying to get under your skin." An awkward silence filled the air before I coughed and continued. I was going to get bruised from that outburst and bratty fib alone. "But, I think she could be a good fit for us, based on her profile."

He stared at me, analyzing.

I stared back at him, plainly.

I meant every damn word.

He handed me the phone. "Alright. Show her to me."

"Yeah?"

"I want to see what you're talking about. Then we'll see if it's something to proceed forward with."

A genuine smile lit my features, and for the first time all day, I saw Aiden visibly relax.

It only made me happier.

I wanted to tell him I loved him, but I didn't even have a chance to do so before his mouth was on mine, my phone now pinned between our chests.

I groaned loudly as his tongue prodded at my mouth, and his own groan reverberated through me as our tongues swiped at each other. I moved my arms fast, clutching his head and raking my hands through his hair.

He pulled away after mere moments, and I all but whined at the loss of contact.

I needed more.

"What do you want, Wraithe?"

My answer was immediate. "You."

"Me? Or her?"

I blinked at him. That was an unexpected question, and frankly, an unfair one when the only thoughts rolling around through my brain were getting his hands back on me. "I don't know her yet. *We* don't know her."

"That isn't what I asked."

Realization started running through me as my heart began beating far too fast.

That wasn't his general caveman tone he used when filled with any sense of jealousy. Instead, that was the tone he used when he wanted something he didn't know he could have. Something that he thought was impossible.

A chance.

My head quirked to the side as I grabbed his chin with my thumb and pointer finger. I wanted him to genuinely hear my next words as our eyes focused on each other. "I want us. And if that 'us' happens to include a girl who seems to have even more issues than we do...then so be it."

He leaned down to kiss me again. His mouth was gentle and sweet, compared to the rough and feverish tone from mere moments ago. After a few minutes, with the both of us panting and filled with more need, he affectionately rested his head against my own as one of his hands started rubbing my thigh. "Show me our girl."

I chuckled. "Already possessive over her, are we?"

"What's mine is mine. Including you."

I TOSSED and turned for hours upon hours for all the reasons one could possibly think of.

Lumpy pillows? *Check.*

Feeling way hotter than I should have? *Check.*

The afternoon sunlight peeking out from behind the blackout curtains that didn't fit the window properly? *Check.*

Not to mention, anxiety was blooming in my stomach. A part of me hoped that my phone would just spontaneously combust so I wouldn't have to open the notifications that may or may not have been there from my lonely actions of yesterday.

*Preyless.*

An absolute act of desperation for some kind of human companionship. In the form of…a kink app. With anonymous strangers. Who may or may not want to kill me. Because who *the fuck* actually knows any of their intentions?

*Maybe you'll be into that next, too*, my subconscious whispered to me.

The bitch.

It wasn't completely wrong, though.

I groaned after flipping over my pillow for the millionth time that afternoon. Knowing sleep was genuinely never going to present itself to me, I grabbed my phone and squinted against the harsh, bright light that illuminated from my phone screen.

7:34 p.m.

My eyes widened in shock. Either I had slept more than I thought, or I had, once again, escaped time through a bubble of dissociation.

Considering my body ached with exhaustion, I went with the second option.

Scrubbing at my eyes wearily, I ripped the Band-Aid off and unlocked my phone, immediately opening the app of pending doom. To my surprise, there were six messages waiting for me.

Immaturely, my heart grew warm at the sight.

I sighed.

God, I was pathetic as ever.

For a girl who made a profile on a kink app, requesting for a random man to dress up and hunt her down before fucking her senseless, and *maybe* keep her after that—all laid out in her bio—it was disturbing how butterflies flew around at the thought of someone merely wanting to talk to me.

And that feeling was made ever worse by the fact that the majority of the messages were even more pitiful than

I was.

That was something I should have expected, given it was literally an anonymous sex app. But I still felt the slightest bit foolish for feeling any sort of dopamine over the attention, when what awaited me was just a slightly spicier version of a dating app.

> **AnonymousDaddy204**
> Hi, Kitten. Need a daddy? You're beautiful.

My nose wrinkled. *No thanks.* Anyone who called themselves "Daddy" without earning the title or honorific, probably had the penis of a frat boy taking steroids.

I deleted the message before moving onto the next one.

> **HotterThanYour3x**
> ur ex never did it rite, i got the zip ties n snacks babe

His username got a snort. But one quick look at his profile, showcasing nothing but cages, collars, and animal ears, made me delete the message as fast as the first one.

To each their own, but that was definitely not for me.

Even if he was correct—I never got snacks. *Was that an option?*

The next set of messages had usernames and openings that one would absolutely expect from such a platform.

**69King4Life**
U into some freaky shit. Me next.

**Will3atYou0ut4Tacos**
On a scale of 1-10, how horny are you
right now?

**FutureStepDad3081**
I'm not saying I'm daddy…but I am
saying you look adoptable.

**TaterThot**
Call me Mr. Potato Head…because
I'm ready to mash

The scowl on my face could have been tattooed on.
Delete, delete, delete, and delete.

Alright, the last guy did make me chuckle, but he was absolutely not the vibe I was looking for with my darker interests.

I didn't want to fuck a potato.

"God," I muttered to myself. "I should have just downloaded Ponder to get laid."

Right as I was about to close the app and get started on the day, another message came in. I had half a mind to delete it on demand and deactivate my profile already, but the words in the chat bubble made me pause before I could.

**PreyForUs**
'PetalstoFangs,' huh? Is there any
meaning to that?

Shrugging, I decided to answer. At least that one had decent grammar, and I really didn't want to get ready for work just yet. Worst case scenario, I could just block them if they turned out to be as lame as the previous usernames, anyway.

> **PetalstoFangs**
> You could say that. I don't think I'm the same girl I was from a few years ago. Reinventing myself, I suppose.

Their response was immediate.

> **PreyForUs**
> I don't think any of us are the same person we were years ago. Life has a way of doing that to us.
>
> What's your story?

> **PetalstoFangs**
> My story? What do you mean?

> **PreyForUs**
> Yeah. Why aren't you the same girl you used to be? I can get popcorn for the lore if it would make you feel better. Or we can exchange stories.
>
> I'll show you mine if you show me yours ;)

I snorted at that one. I never thought I would receive that in the context of trauma.

It also made me smile that this human used the term "lore," too.

Whoever I was talking to definitely passed the vibe check, more than ever.

Sighing, I decided to go with a lacking but truthful answer.

> **PetalstoFangs**
> Got in a relationship with the wrong kind of man. I haven't known peace since.

> **PreyForUs**
> Are you still with said man?

> **PetalstoFangs**
> I am not.

> **PreyForUs**
> Good. I'm not afraid of getting my hands dirty.

That made me smile as I typed up my next message.
It almost felt protective.
I liked it.
Even if it was from a stranger who could do absolutely nothing about it.

> **PetalstoFangs**
> Oh, yeah? What does that mean?

> **PreyForUs**
> Ah, ah, darlin'. We may be on a kink app, but the FBI still have their ways. I'll keep that one to myself for now.

I blinked.

That shouldn't have been hot. But it absolutely was.

> **PetalstoFangs**
> Alright. I showed you mine. Your turn.

> Dear God, don't send me a dick pic yet. I'm exhausted and will bite it off.

I needed sex, sure, but I was still a lady, after all.

> **PreyForUs**
> Feisty. Wasn't on the agenda, though.

> What do you want to know? We're an open book, pretty girl.

My eyebrows scrunched together at his usage of the word "we're," and I quickly clicked on his profile to read more about the man I was talking to.

Or...men, I realized.

I could have face palmed myself then and there.

That would have explained why their username had the word "us" in it, too.

Fucking *duh*.

I really needed to sleep for another twenty-four hours.

My eyes scanned down their profile for more information, and my heart could have exploded at the amount of kinks we had in common.

**PreyForUs is into:** BDSM power dynamics (dominant), breath play, breeding, collaring, cosplay, double penetration, double vaginal penetration, exhibitionism, fear play, kidnapping, light pain, mask play, non-con, orgasm control, ownership, pegging, polyamory, primal (hunting/predator), sex toys, somnophilia, and weapon play.

**PreyForUs is maybe-into:** Blood, bruising, DD/LG, fisting, hypnotism, sensory deprivation, and squirting/cum play.

**PreyForUs is not-into:** Chastity, cheating, gangbang, glory hole, pet play, self-humiliation (both sides), sharing outside dynamic, and tickling.

I didn't know if I should have been blushing, hiding, or falling down at their feet for all of the information presented in front of me.

I was overwhelmed, for sure.

But in that exact same breath, they were exactly what I was looking for. And I was more than curious to learn more about them. I clicked on their general information next, skimming over their location—Antarctica, code for anonymous—and bio.

**PreyForUs Bio:** M(34)/M(36) couple seeking a third (F). East coast. Preference to long-term dynamic addition. Kinks are listed below for compatibility. Military-based, so we ask for patience in communication through text.

I jumped as another message came in.

**PreyForUs**
Don't tell me we scared you away
already. We didn't even get into the
lore. XD

**PetalstoFangs**
LOL. No, I was reading your profile. I
have to know who could be on their
way over to murder me, you know.

So, there's two of you? Which one am
I speaking with?

**PreyForUs**
I don't think you'd be too sad if we
hunted you down, darlin'.

And we're both talking to you. We live
together.

**PetalstoFangs**
Quite the opposite, in complete
honesty.

**PreyForUs**
That's the only question you have
for us?

**PetalstoFangs**
No. But why rush through all the good
stuff? Unless either of you are just
looking for a quick jerk-off. In which
case, I'm sure some other girl would
love to help you out.

> **PreyForUs**
> Oh, pretty girl. Believe me. You're intriguing, and a single quick jerk-off would not be fulfilling for either of us whatsoever.

> **PetalstoFangs**
> I just blushed.

> **PreyForUs**
> I wonder how far down that blush goes.

> I wonder if you'd enjoy us tracing it down. With our tongues…or worse.

I nearly choked on my own spit at that response. Whoever these men were—they were already showing themselves to be possessive, and it made my heart go pitter-patter.

A red flag to the majority of society.

But exactly what I had been craving.

Except...

> **PetalstoFangs**
> What do you both look like? Your profile didn't have that. I could be talking to a lonely eighty-year-old woman for all I know.

The photo came in immediately, and choking on my spit was no longer a concern given how my mouth dried up instantly. Their faces were cropped out of the shot—understandable, given the nature of the app and our anonymous identities—but their bodies were more than enough to fawn over.

Muscles upon muscles. Six packs. Biceps. Even their thighs were muscular.

And God…

They were tattooed.

Tattoos were my weakness. It could be a butterfly tattoo on a man's pelvis, for all I cared.

I, unashamedly, would have still probably licked it.

**PetalstoFangs**
Yeah…definitely not a lonely woman. My God. I almost just dropped my phone.

**PreyForUs**
Afraid not, pretty girl.

You okay over there?

**PetalstoFangs**
Nope.

I glanced at the time on the phone screen and cursed.

**PetalstoFangs**
I need to get ready for work, unfortunately. I'm sorry.

**PreyForUs**
So soon? We didn't actually scare you off, did we?

> **PetalstoFangs**
> Absolutely not. Generally, I'd love to talk to you throughout my desolate night-shift activities, but my boss will be here tonight. And he kinda… doesn't believe in cellphones, even if he means well.

> **PreyForUs**
> *laughing emoji*

> Enjoy your shift. We'll be here.

> Oh, and darlin'? Turn your location off in the settings. That's unsafe as all hell, and anyone could find you if they have the skills to do so. Including us.

A normal girl would have deactivated their account from that message alone.

But me? I smiled.

That was exactly what I wanted.

I had been married to an abusive man who did terrible things to me. A man who made me suck on guns for nothing but the cruel intention of hurting me. A man who forced me to run through the woods and hide, or else there would be hell to pay. A complete and utter psychopath. The kind of man who would never be missed, and when that drunk driver hit him...I felt nothing except relief.

Even if that meant I'd rot in hell with him.

And yet, through my healing journey and therapy sessions, I had learned that I craved what he did to me then more than ever.

That danger. That psychotic, yet lusting hunt.

But...on my terms.

As I went into my settings to turn my location off—appeasing them, for the moment—I only hoped that they did, indeed, possess those scary tracking skills.

Because I already knew that I would let them keep me as their desired third if they tracked me down.

# FOUR

RORY

"FUCKING...RUN," Trent whispered in my ear as I stared out at the wilderness surrounding our townhome. My body quivered in the freezing February air, the chill from the nonstop rain in Seattle doing very little to curb the rod of ice that was starting to coat my spine.

It also didn't help that I was in nothing but a lacy bra and panties.

His favorite set.

My response was barely audible over the clattering of my teeth. "Please don't make me do this."

His responding chuckle was all I needed to know that I wasn't going to get out of it.

It was my punishment, after all.

I fell asleep too early, and his dinner got cold.

It didn't matter that he had come home two hours later than expected, smelling like various kinds of mixed liquor.

It was still my fault.

That liquor scented voice started again, right as I felt the cold barrel of a pistol at my temple. "I told you to run. This is what I like. If you can't handle that, I can always end our marriage right here. It's not like you're useful to me, anyway. Huh? Since you refuse to give me what I really want."

I shook. I couldn't tell if it was from the utmost fear cursing through my veins, the adrenaline, or the cold. It had to be a mixture of everything.

Tears lined my eyes. I refused to look anywhere but in front of me. "Why do you hate me? What did I do?"

The safety of the gun clicking off made my eyes widen, and disgust rolled through me as he wrapped a hand around my waist, only to reach up and fondle one of my boobs roughly. "Can't you see, baby? I love you. This is how I show my love. Now, be a good puppy, and run. I'm not going to ask again."

At the declaration of his love, I swallowed roughly and kicked off in a run, knowing what was going to come next.

I was going to lose yet another part of myself. At a meager twenty-years-old.

And I was going to wish my husband dead the entire time.

"ARE YOU ALRIGHT, SWEETHEART?" JOHN'S voice sounded, effectively snapping me out of the terrible memory that often showed itself when I was exhausted.

The memory of the night that shattered me in more ways than I expected.

I shook my head as I looked at the old man standing across from me. "Just tired. I'll be okay, though."

"Girly, you know better than to bullshit me at this point. What's going on?"

I chuckled. He had me there.

In the year I had been working for John, we had somehow grown closer with each passing night, as it was the only time he ever stepped foot in his own hotel. He claimed he preferred the quiet to do paperwork and the bookkeeping, but considering he was in once, sometimes even twice a week, I had the sneaking suspicion he just needed someone to talk to every now and then.

Especially after Mary's passing months ago.

I didn't mind it, though.

There were times I equally needed someone to talk to.

Being lonely was almost as debilitating as being lost, if they didn't already coincide.

I dropped my faux, placating smile. "Can I ask you something personal?"

He raised an eyebrow and leaned against the check-in counter before crossing his arms. It was a humoring sight, to say the least, considering he fit all the bills of the signature "old man look." From his blue, button-down shirt and his khaki pants, to his white, slicked-back hair and unruly mustache—there was no mistaking the life experience he carried. He responded, "Go on…"

"Have you ever had something bad happen to you… only for you to crave it happening again? Like, you shouldn't want that. It damaged you. But you also don't remember who you were before it all?"

Understanding lit his face. "You thinking about him again?"

"Unfortunately."

"I can't say I've been in your shoes, girly. You met Mary. She was the love of my life, and I would have done anything for her." He smiled sadly, and I nodded, urging him to continue. "But I can say that I have hit terrible lows in this life. And while I absolutely never want to experience them again…there is somehow comfort in the silence and solace of misery when it was all that you knew of, once upon a time. So, I don't crave it, but I also understand it."

I swallowed roughly and turned away from him as I asked my next question. I had to beat around the bush, as I was absolutely *not* talking to John about my sex life. But my therapy appointment was still a week out, and I needed the answer then. "Say you found a way to potentially take control of the situation, though. Finding comfort in the misery…but on your terms. Would that make it better?"

"I would think so. As long as you're not actually putting yourself in genuine danger."

I almost wanted to laugh.

That was, unfortunately, the kicker.

I had no fucking idea.

What I was doing…What I wanted to find on *Prey-less*? It was dangerous as fuck.

I wanted strangers to hurt me—to hunt me down, like a cat with a mouse—and there was no telling how I would react once it happened.

You could only rely on porn so much for confirmation of likes and dislikes.

Add trauma into the equation?

You might as well be making an atomic bomb.

Or…you could be creating the cure for insanity.

He started again, "Should I be worried, Rory? Is there someone wanting to hurt you? Or are you wanting to hurt yourself?"

I turned to him quickly. "No! God, no. I don't even know if they actually want anything to do with me. You know my brain, though. Overthinking-central."

John blinked. "'They'?"

Oh, fuck me.

I went to answer, blushing and stuttering on my breath, before he raised a hand and cut me off. "I don't wanna know. Just tell me this—are you being safe? And not just…ya know, health-class safe? But *actually* safe?"

My mind raced like a hamster on a wheel.

The truthful answer was…no. I knew I wasn't being safe.

But he didn't need to know that.

I smiled, lying through my teeth. "Of course."

He nodded to himself before turning toward his office. My heart rate accelerated as he spoke again. "You're a bullshit liar, sweetheart. It's alright, though. I have a shotgun with more than enough rounds for whatever definition a 'they' requires. Let me know if we need it."

I laughed loudly. "No being arrested, John!"

He scoffed. "Girly, I am old as shit *and* a widow. They'd just take pity on me at this point."

IMMEDIATELY UPON ENTERING MY MAKESHIFT apartment, I reached for my phone, desperate to check and see if the mystery military men had responded.

My heart sped up as I saw multiple messages.

> **PreyForUs**
> Hope you're having a good shift!
>
> What kind of old man doesn't believe in cellphones anymore? Lame.
>
> I don't think we told you this btw…but you're beautiful, and you deserve to be told that.
>
> I don't feel like going to sleep yet, but Wolfe (the grumpy one who calls you "pretty girl") is telling me to leave you alone. Ugh.

I chuckled before realizing that the last message came through only ten minutes ago.

What the fuck were they doing awake through the night?

I thought military men had to wake up at the crack of dawn. Not go to sleep.

Collapsing on the bed, my fingers started to move.

> **PetalstoFangs**
> Why the hell are you awake at all?

> **PreyForUs**
> We had to make sure our future wife was safe and sound. Duh.

I blushed.
I should not have liked that.
Oh well.

> **PetalstoFangs**
> Aren't you two married already? And damn, at least buy a girl flowers before you buy her a ring.

> **PreyForUs**
> *eyeroll emoji*
>
> No, we're not married yet. But even if we were to get married tomorrow, our future third will still be referred to everyone as our wife. Even if it's technically illegal for official certification.

My eyes were growing heavy as I started typing out my response.

> **PetalstoFangs**
> Are you wanting me as your third?
> Sounds like a big decision for just
> meeting.

> **PreyForUs**
> Well…I mean, maybe. We'd need to
> cover a few things first.

> The real question is—are you open to
> something like this?

> Wolfe wants me to tell you that there's
> no pressure, but I think he's lying.

A LAUGH BUBBLED OUT OF ME.

> **PetalstoFangs**
> I think so. I'm not against it, anyway.
> I've read books with weirder things
> happening, so, I mean *shrugging
> emoji* It's up for discussion.

> But I need something before I say yes,
> officially.

Minutes passed.

I was quickly losing the battle for sleep.

Thankfully, though, the feeling of my phone buzzing against my chest forced my eyes open again.

> **PreyForUs**
> What do you need?

> And how can we make that happen for
> you?

# FIVE

"FUCK," I ground out through clenched teeth as Casey bobbed his head up and down the length of my cock. He had wasted absolutely no time in unbuckling my belt and pulling my briefs and pants down my legs—where they then sat, still wrapped around my ankles—after PetalstoFang's response sprung my dick to life. "You didn't even give me a chance to respond. Holy shit."

He only moaned around my dick, forcing my back to arch as it vibrated every nerve ending in me. It was made both better and worse when he added his hand to the mix by perfectly stroking up and down my length, the spit acting as lube, and I swore that I could already feel my balls begin to tingle.

The phone with her messages was quickly put on the back burner.

Just for a few moments, anyway.

I fisted his hair in a firm grasp before leaning back

slightly and shoving his head down. He gagged brutally, his throat constricting on all eight inches of me. My chest all but vibrated as I forced him to keep it down for four full seconds. "Yeah? You wanted to be eager, Wraithe. So be a good fucking boy and take a face-fucking then. *Eagerly.*"

Once the four seconds were up, I relinquished my hold on his head and watched as he came up for air. His eyes were lined with tears, and spit still connected my dick to his pouty mouth.

God, how I loved that sight.

"You..." he panted, "are a caveman."

I chuckled darkly as I grabbed the base of my cock and smacked it against his pouty lips. "You complaining, pretty boy?"

"Never."

"Get back to it, then."

He didn't even hesitate. Once again, his mouth was sucking my dick down his throat—that time, without me even having to force it. He took me all the way down, forcing past his own barrier. I groaned as I felt him swallow, only to somehow lick my balls, too.

Fuck me.

That alone was one reason I probably fell in love with him.

Because that was a fucking talent.

I growled. "Wraithe. Godfuckingdamnit. More...just a little more."

Instead of giving me more, though, the brat popped his head off my cock again. His eyes landed on my phone.

"Better answer our girl, Daddy. She's gonna think we're not interested."

Despite the warring emotions of wanting to get off, I also wanted to respond to our girl. So I nodded and reached for my phone.

I knew he was right.

Even if my heartbeat was literally in my cock.

Except, when my eyes scanned Petals' last set of text messages once again, I watched as precum built at the crown of my dick. Which Casey licked at immediately, making me groan.

> **PetalstoFangs**
> I mentioned it to you both already, but I was previously married to a bad man. He made me do things I didn't want to do. But now, I actually want to do those things. Just like my bio suggests. I want a dominant man—or, well…men—to enact a scene similar to what I used to do. But I want to enjoy it this time.

My heart panged at that message. That certainly didn't get me hard in the slightest.

Whatever she had gone through—it had fucked her up for life.

And I felt bad for her.

But in that same breath, I wanted to prove Casey right and beat my chest like a caveman when her next message came through immediately after.

It was her next set of messages that led me to getting my dick sucked.

> **PetalstoFangs**
>
> I've done my research. I want to live out a primal scene. I don't necessarily care how it begins, or how it ends. But I wanted to be hunted, scared, and completely out of control of the situation.

> I've watched some pornos with it, too. Ranging from CNC to just typical sex. Masks are hot. Knives are hotter. My only real hard limit for that kind of scene is guns and anal without lube.

> God. Even admitting this to you both is getting me hot.

*Ding, ding, ding.*

Boner.

"Suck. Finger my ass while you're down there too, pretty boy. Make me come," I ordered as I turned my hooded gaze toward Wraithe and started typing again. At that point, I realized she could have fallen asleep, but I was crossing my fingers that it wasn't the case.

> **PreyForUs**
>
> Naughty girl. This is something I've actually wanted to do for some time, though. With another female, that is. I've done something similar with Wraithe already.

Her response was immediate. *Thank fuck.* I knew she had to be tired.

**PetalstoFangs**
Yeah? Really?

What would you do? If you could?

> **PreyForUs**
> Wraithe and I would surprise you at your job. You would get a text from one of us, telling you to go out into the parking lot. I'd recommend telling your boss or coworker that you're ill and need to go home.

**PetalstoFangs**
Okay…

> **PreyForUs**
> Then we would simply make that fantasy come true. Maybe I sneak up from behind you and put a hand to your mouth. Fuck, maybe I put a drug-coated rag to your mouth instead and force you to breathe it in. Maybe I make you take the lead before I strip the control from you entirely. Regardless, you'd belong to us for the night.

**PetalstoFangs**
Oh my God.

Don't stop. Please.

> **PreyForUs**
> Then we'd either drag you or drive you to some remote woods. And we would tell you to run. And you will do just that.

> And when we catch you, we fuck you.

> You say it'd be against your will, but I'd bet money you'd be dripping for us.

> I bet you're dripping now, aren't you?

Typing out that last sentence, I moaned loudly as Casey dragged his teeth over my length, right as he pushed two fingers in my ass. My eyes darted to him, and we both watched as my cock visibly twitched from the motions of him fingering me.

"Baby," I groaned out. "Fuck, yes. God, I love you. I love what you do to me."

He looked up at me and whimpered.

Fucking...whimpered.

Just at my words.

Goddamn.

I continued. "I want to come. Suck the cum out of my balls, Wraithe. C'mon. I know you can do it, baby."

"Say please," he muttered, smirking.

I shook my head before fisting his hair once again, guiding his mouth right back to my length. He was the only person I had ever begged for, but I'd beg a thousand times over for anything regarding him. "Please, pretty boy."

Just like that, he went after my fucking soul with renewed effort. His fingers fucked my puckered hole, hard, knuckles deep and curling toward my prostate, as he deepthroated me again and again. Repeatedly, his nose brushed against my pubic bone as he took me all the way down, and I felt my balls draw up tight.

At that moment, my phone buzzed, and I forced myself to look at it instead of him.

The sight had me yanking Casey's head off of me.

I held his hair tightly, groaning roughly as my cum spurted out and landed all over his face. Rope after rope of my seed hit him, and I groaned even louder as he stuck his tongue out, trying to catch everything he could. His fist continued pumping at my length, milking me for everything I had, and heat flew all the way from my head to my toes at the sensation.

I looked back down at my phone, nearly slumping over.

**PetalstoFangs**

...I came from that alone.

*one attached image*

At the cusp of my orgasm, Petals had sent me a fucking picture of her fingers—wet, sticky, and covered in her own cum.

All from me merely telling her a brief plan about what we would do to her.

I swallowed roughly.

I guess I had a type—eager and reactive.

Casey moved his mouth back to the tip of my cock, and I huffed as he sucked my sensitive tip again—still covered in my cum.

Then...an idea hit me.

I grabbed his head and opened my camera app.

Making sure to cut off the top part of his face—for the time being, at least—I snapped the shot of my softening dick in his mouth, and all the visible proof of my orgasm on his face.

He released my dick with a soft pop. "Are you sending that to her?"

I nodded. "She wanted to play with fire. Now she's going to get burnt."

> **PreyForUs**
> So did I.
>
> *one attached image*

Once that was sent, I nearly threw my phone to the side, kicked the clothes around my ankles off, grabbed Casey's hand, and drug him to our bedroom.

He laughed as he followed me. "What're we doing?"

I turned back to him with a smirk. "You really think I'm not gonna make you finish after that? I'm going to make you scream for your Daddy. And then we're going to go get our fucking girl and erase the memory of whatever that sick fuck did to her, by doing it how she'll like it."

# SIX

"HI!" My voice came out chipper, which was surprising even to myself considering I was anything but. Instead...I could have sworn my blood was *itchy*. "Welcome to the Wooded Lodg—"

"Yeah," the man in front of me said, effectively cutting me off and throwing his debit card on the counter. He was dressed in board shorts and a tank top, with sand from the beach still covering nearly every area of exposed skin on him. "One room, one night, one bed, please."

A woman nearly identical to my height stood in his embrace, wearing nothing but a yellow bikini and flip flops. Unsurprising, considering she was also covered in sand and was utterly soaked.

Sigh.

At least he said please.

Even if the sand mixture covering the both of them

from their apparent midnight swimming was dripping *everywhere.*

I nodded politely and began typing the information into the computer in front of me. After a minute or so, the man sighed exasperatedly. "Anything?"

My eyes snapped to him, irritated. "The system is loading."

"Can it load faster? I have a long night ahead. I mean, look at her."

My face rolled in disgust at the innuendo behind his words. I was thankful that there were no microphones on the surveillance cameras...and also for the fact that John had all but adopted me since I had started working there. He had just begun some sort of paperwork in the back-room, but even so—my smart mouth would have prob-ably been congratulated rather than disciplined if he overheard me. "Let me guess. Brad? Kyle? Justin, even?"

His mouth parted in shock. "...Justin, yes. Do I know you?"

"No." I shook my head. "You just look like the douchebag type who loves intimidating women for no reason other than, '*oooh, highscore, woman scared,*' and 'J' names are common for such *creatures*. Unfortunately for you, I've met men who make you look like a worm, so...I am not intimidated in the slightest, and if you'll let me do my job, then we'll get you on your way very shortly. *Mkay?* Mkay."

The woman tucked under his arm coughed, and I had the suspicion she was biting back a laugh, which only filled me with satisfaction. When my eyes floated up to meet the man's gaze for confirmation that he had actually heard me, the satisfaction only grew at the sign of his blushing, embarrassed complexion.

Rory: 1

Weird Men: 0

To his credit, he stayed silent, and I smiled sarcastically before returning my gaze to the computer in front of me. I reached for a keycard, magnetizing it for usage, and spoke again. "You're in luck. We have one last room available on the third floor. Beautiful view, too."

He nodded. "You have an elevator, right?"

I forced the faux wince on my face as I handed him his debit card and the hotel keycard. "I'm so sorry, sir, but our elevator is currently out of order. Our stairs are on the right of that left wall, though."

He scowled as he walked to the stairwell, tugging his guest along. "Of course it is."

As I watched him all but drag her, I almost felt bad for the poor girl.

Especially since their window faced the parking lot, rather than the beach.

Collateral damage, unfortunately.

I could only hope that he at least lasted in bed.

Doubtful.

I shrugged as I returned my gaze to the computer, resetting the search and availability setting, and turning behind me to keep note on the recently updated third-shift checklist. Trying to keep my mind busy as much as I possibly could.

It didn't do much, though.

Unsurprising, given that night was technically *the* night.

Either my walking fantasy was going to come to life... or I was going to leave *Preyless* and the kink scene entirely and continue going to proper therapy. Granted, there was nothing wrong with my therapist, and I'd be returning to hear more of his guidance even if everything went in the direction I wanted it to. I just...simply refused to try again with another man who could turn the tables on me, should it all have failed. And with what I wanted? A failure and ghosting would have just been a sign from God.

It had been nearly two weeks of conversations with the men I had taken an extreme liking to on that dumb app since the morning I had gotten off to the thoughts of a proper scene.

Two weeks of planning, but also, two weeks of growing to trust and like them.

Romantic feelings were genuinely growing toward them.

They made me smile, blush, and swoon more than I ever had in my entire life—let alone more than I ever had throughout my entire marriage.

Not to mention...the orgasms that racked through my body at their promised words—both threatening and sensual—had me wholly addicted.

Porn already didn't compare. Frankly, it was terrify-ing, considering I didn't know their names or what their voices sounded like. And yet, I was still craving more.

My phone sat heavy in my back pocket as I wondered about the men. If I should text them to confirm or if I should throw my phone into the goddamn ocean. If they actually like-liked me, like they said they did, or if they were just placating me until they found someone better for their needs.

Just like that, my thoughts began to spiral. Again.

Until the clearing of a throat softly filled the air, signaling the need for my attention. I turned and blinked in shock, and all thoughts flew directly out of my skull.

An unbelievably attractive man—who I hadn't even known was there. Who had probably been watching me twiddle my fingers and buzz anxiously for who knows how long. And who quite literally towered over me even with the desk in between us.

Just great.

I wanted to facepalm. "H-hello!" I stuttered out. "I'm so sorry. My head is everywhere tonight. What can I do for you?"

He smirked down at me as he handed me his keycard. "It's no problem. I have a card holder on my phone, and like a dumbass, I slid this in with the mixture of it and all of the RFID tags in my wallet. I think it's demagnetized now. We can't get in our room."

"Oh! That's no problem. What's your name? I can look you up and repair the data."

"Aiden West. It could also be under my boyfriend's name. Casey Bennett."

I nodded as I typed their names into the system. Thankfully, it popped right up under the first name, and I looked through their information to find their assigned room right as he spoke again. "How's your night going so far?"

I smiled up at him. "Not many complaints, other

than a lot of sand to clean up now. How about yourself?"

He looked down at the floor and grimaced. "I noticed. That sucks. Are you here alone? Is there anyone else that could help?"

I shook my head. "The owner is in the back tonight, but I'm sure I'll be the one cleaning it up. It just comes with working on the beach. What can you do, ya know?"

"Well, if it was the guy who was rude to you earlier, then I like you even more for telling him the elevator was broken when it's not. Considering I just used it."

My eyes nearly popped out of my head. "Have you been here for that long?"

"Yup. That was very clever actually. I had debated tripping him on the way to the elevator but you beat me to it."

I laughed as I returned my gaze to the computer, only for them to return to him after quickly repairing his keycard. I locked eyes with him, handing it back before centering my pointer finger on my lips in a faux shushing motion. "Don't tell my boss."

He tapped his fingers on the desk and winked before turning toward the exit. "Your secret is safe with me, pretty girl."

I felt like a lightning bolt hit me as I blinked in shock.

That nickname...

Right on cue, the elevator dinged, and another man walked out. He was nearly as tall as the one who had just stood before me. As he approached the front desk in a matching black hoodie and shorts, nervousness bloomed in my stomach tenfold.

The hoodies had the Navy SEAL emblem on the breast-pocket area.

Holy shit.

The man from the elevator smiled at me before placing a bouquet of flowers on the desk. It was only then that I realized he had been carrying them, or that his other hand was carrying a heavy duffel bag. "Good evening, darlin'. Just wanted to keep that promise of getting you flowers first. Being chivalrous is important in a relationship, ya know."

My face stayed frozen.

Wolfe and Wraithe.

The man standing near the exit spoke again, and I jumped, realizing he hadn't left yet. "Casey, babe, c'mon. We gotta get ready."

*Casey* winked, just like *Aiden* had, and I watched as they left the building without a backward glance. It wasn't even a full sixty seconds later when my phone buzzed in my back pocket, forcing me to nearly jump out of my skin.

**PreyForUs**
We wanted to give you our real names
and faces to make sure you felt safe.

Give us five minutes.

You know what to do after that, pretty
girl. If you still want this. Last chance
to back out.

I looked at the clock. 11:12 p.m.

Regardless of my nerves, I didn't hesitate.

It was really happening.

They came.

I watched the clock for an entire five minutes, drumming my fingers along the desk anxiously. And when the exact second turned the clock to 11:17, I slid my phone back into my pocket, walked into John's office with a claim that I felt extremely ill and needed to leave, and followed my *Preyless* men right out of the building, into the darkness.

Just like we had planned.

# SEVEN

## CASEY

WE BOTH SAT COMPLETELY STILL, silent and watching, as our girl walked to the tree line.

I had to swallow down my grunt.

Our girl.

God, that did things to me, and it was only just the beginning. There was absolutely no telling how feral I would become for this beautiful woman as time went on. From her crystal-blue eyes to her pin-straight black hair, all the way down to her French-tip-painted toes we had seen in a recent mirror selfie.

Aiden may have been the caveman when there was only two of us, but I feared that girl would be dealing with two cavemen very shortly.

Because, regardless of how that night went...Petalsto-Fangs was our girl.

Aiden waved his hand in front of my face—the asshole—to snap me out of my thoughts. I turned to look at him with an exasperated eyeroll and raised my brow since the balaclava hid any other part of my face. Good thing, too, or else I would have stuck my tongue out at him. I was already antsy after someone caught us changing from our civilian clothes into uniforms in a random parking lot, let alone our plans for the night.

His face, however, wasn't masked-up like mine was, and the stern glare and set jaw that followed my petulant eyeroll was focused on me. He raised his hand again, using two fingers to show where our girl had entered the forest, and I hissed under my breath.

Go time.

As silent as the night, I stood and began trekking after her. My footsteps were light and precise, unlike the man behind me who somehow clomped around like a beast unless he was careful. But even if I was the stealthy one, Aiden was the hunter—and it was more than useful. In duty, it was the exact same way. We may as well have been treating the beginning of that night as if it were a mission. It was why he had the night vision headset on instead of the concealing mask I wore.

I smirked at the thought.

Our little doe really didn't realize who she had gotten involved with.

She would soon, though.

Even without the night vision headset, picking her out of the dark was exceptionally easy. Somehow, her hair was so dark that the moon's light bounced off it, making it look like she had a halo. And she was mere feet away.

I swallowed roughly and planted myself behind a

tree, hidden from her sight, before I spoke. "You really didn't hide as well as I thought you would have, darlin'."

The yelp that came out of her throat at the sound of my voice was intoxicating.

Her voice trembled as she spoke. "I didn't know we were playing hide and seek."

"We're not, but that does sound very intriguing for next time."

"N-next time? Where even are you?"

Ignoring her first question—because *yes*, next time—I picked up a small shell that had somehow gotten to the tree line and tossed it. I moved my head slightly from behind the tree to see where it landed and smiled glee-fully when I saw it at her feet.

She stared down at the shell. "That doesn't answer my question."

My tone was full of mock pout. "Awe. I guess it doesn't. Tell you what...how about we play the game of 'Warmer, Colder,' before the real game begins. If you win, you get to tell us how the rest of the night is going to go. But if you lose, then you're ours to do whatever we want with. Yeah?"

I bit my lip as I watched her mull it over. She crossed her arms, rubbing them against the chill before nodding. "Okay. Yeah."

Satisfaction warred through me. *Good girl.*

Even if I wouldn't let her win.

"Go on," I urged. "Start walking. Follow the sound of my voice."

She did just that, and I had to bite back my laugh as

she walked in the complete opposite direction. She was going to be so much fun.

I trailed after her so my voice wouldn't carry too much and ruin the game. "Warmer."

She paused, shifting to the left.

"Colder."

She immediately huffed and went to the right instead. I smirked as I watched her stomp around the woods. The October leaves crunched around her, and like clockwork, the light sounds of Aiden's footsteps followed as he entered the tree line with us. When I felt him right next to me, I called out to her again, eager to frustrate her now. "Colder!"

Aiden turned his head to look at me with a smirk.

Being a brat was exceptionally useful when it came to other brats.

We watched as she threw her arms up and started walking right back toward us. "I have a feeling you're not playing very fair, Wraithe."

I laughed. "How'd you know it was me playing the game?"

I watched as her head turned quizzically, noting where my voice was actually coming from, before she began tiptoeing toward me.

Our little doe thought she was sneaky. It was adorable.

She poked her head around a tree. "You're the one who calls me 'darlin'.' Wolfe calls me 'pretty girl.' Where is he in all of this?"

Aiden spoke for me that time, and the smirk coating his voice was beyond laughable. "Oh, I'm here, pretty girl. We really gotta talk about your wardrobe choice for running around in the woods, though. A T-shirt and shorts? You're gonna be walking out of here bloody."

I bit my lip to stifle my groan.

Hot.

Her head poked around another tree, and I signaled to Aiden to stay put as I began setting up the real trap. He knew exactly what I was going to do without me saying it and smiled thankfully.

Our doe spoke again. "Maybe I want that."

I spoke next. "We know. Doesn't mean you won't walk away with a red ass for the choice."

"Y-you'd s-spank me for that?"

"Yes," I stated. It wasn't even up for discussion. If anyone was going to make her bleed, it was going to be us. Not the underbrush of trees and dead bushes. "You're getting a nice version of us tonight, though. We're not going to make you run—just yet. We're not going to punish you, either. This game is a good starting point. Alright?"

"Ye-yes. Okay."

Aiden spoke next. "Warmer."

She nodded to herself and took a few more steps toward his voice.

She was within two yards of him when he spoke again. "You're so warm, pretty girl."

My own dick twitched at the warmth coating his tone. That was the tone that had me calling him Daddy, and it made me want to hear her call him that, too.

I shook the thought out of my head.

The absolute last thing I wanted to do was leak in my camo before the fun had even begun.

I had to get control of my thoughts.

Going off of that, I slowly unclasped the dagger from my belt and watched as she got even closer to Aiden. Taking a deep breath, I walked toward her stealthily, and my gloved hand covered her mouth seconds later. She screamed against me as I raised the knife up to her line of vision, only to lower it and cut her shirt right down the middle. She thrashed slightly as I did so, forcing me to cut into the soft skin of her abdomen, and I cursed under my breath.

Blood didn't scare me in the slightest, but that didn't mean I necessarily wanted to make her bleed...

Yet.

"Easy, darlin'. You're safe. It's just us."

My words soothed her slightly, and her thrashing stopped. Only to turn into trembling.

I kept my hold on her firm all the same.

Aiden walked out from behind the tree to stand in front of us, towering over her as he spoke. "You're on fire, pretty girl."

CASEY'S HAND still covered the entire bottom half of our prey's face; though, it only made me grow stiffer in my uniform as I realized exactly how tiny she was compared to the both of us.

Sure, I noticed it when we were at the hotel.

But now I was right in front of her.

I could touch her. I could smell her. I could *ruin* her.

I moved my eyes to Casey through the headset, only to swallow roughly when I found him already staring at her with nothing but admiration in his eyes.

If this night went exactly how we wanted it to...

I shook my head and swallowed roughly as I stepped even closer to the both of them. It forced Casey to step backwards, dragging her along with him until his back was at another tree while she was pressed firmly against him. Her eyes stayed locked on me, fear and excitement racing through them. "Hi, pretty girl."

Casey groaned. "God, she really is beautiful, isn't she?"

I smirked. *Our* pretty prey.

If it weren't for my night vision headset, and the fact that our doe was still muffled, I would have bet my entire rank that she was blushing as bright as a rose petal.

I took another step forward and twirled a lock of her hair around my gloved hand. "Oh, she really, really is. Even with muddy legs and a ripped up shirt. We haven't even started the chase yet. Imagine how stunning she'll look when she's pinned in the sand and moaning for us like an animal in heat."

"Fuck, Aiden. I'm already trying not to bust in my uniform. Take it easy," Casey whimpered.

One of my eyebrows quirked up as I moved my other hand to cup him. He hissed through his teeth, clutching at our doe even firmer than before, and I could have sworn her legs shifted to cross. Refusing to let that happen though, I raised one of my knees just slightly, angling it directly in between her legs, and swallowed my own groan as she let out a muffled moan in response. "What was that?" I mocked. "*Make you come right here, right now, just to remind you of your place, too?* Because... don't forget, you still answer to me, pretty boy."

His icy eyes fell closed. "Please, no. I'm sorry, Daddy. I want to save it for her. She's earned it."

Pride swelled in my chest.

That was a good answer.

"Good boy," I responded before looking back down to our pretty girl. Testing the boundaries a bit more, I shifted my knee against her core, rubbing it back and forth. She moaned again. I relished in the sound of it, even more so as her eyes closed in submission while she rocked back down on me. "A needy boy and a needy girl, right in front of me. Just aching for that release. How could I have ever gotten so lucky?"

Casey groaned.

I continued. "Casey, sweetheart—move your hand. I want to hear our pretty girl talk. We need to ask her a few things, remember?"

He did so, moving his hand to her waist. I watched her mouth drop open as he pushed her down the slightest bit, forcing her to rock on my knee even harder. My dick twitched at the sight of his hand covering her entire waist and the sound of her practically panting.

The sight unraveled me slightly. I couldn't help myself.

I raised my own hand and stuck two fingers in her mouth. Her eyes snapped wide open as I pressed down on her tongue, forcing her to cough as I explored. I tested the boundaries, pressing against the back of her throat. The guttural sound that escaped me when she didn't gag was nothing short of feral.

Her hips rocked against me even faster as I withdrew my gloved hand, now covered in her spit, and cupped her jaw firmly. "What's your name, beautiful? I think we're at the point you can tell us now."

"Ro-Rory," she moaned out.

Casey groaned. "Rory. Such a pretty name for a darling girl."

I smiled. "It is. Now, Rory—what's your safe word? The one we gave you in the chat when we were discussing tonight. I need you to tell me it so I know you're okay with what's happened so far. Do you understand?"

She nodded. "Flower."

"Good girl. And do you need to say it?"

Her voice turned quiet and shy. "No. I'm okay."

Casey responded for me. "Good. That's wonderful. We trust you'd say it if you needed to, yeah? You won't get in trouble. This is for you, after all. We don't want to hurt you anymore than you want to be hurt."

She nodded, and I took that as my cue to grab the other side of her waist and firmly press her against me. The gasp that tore out of her almost had me kneeling at her feet. "This is what you wanted, right? Two men to hunt you down. Two men to touch you. Two men to make you come. Two men to *own* you."

"Fuck," she ground out. "Fuck, yes. Please. I promise I want this. Words are just...kinda hard right now. I...I didn't think you'd make me feel so good, so early? I don't know."

The laughs that left Casey and my mouth were mocking. "Good girl. And of course we would. Casey is right, after all. You deserve it. You're already making us so proud, little doe."

A sound of pleasure and delirium left her lips. "Yeah?"

"Oh, yes, darling girl. Now, we want you to come like this. Do you think you can do that for us? Come on Aiden's leg while we touch you. Before we've even *really* touched you."

"Oh my God," she whined. "I've never come like this before. I've never..."

I squinted down. I didn't like where that was heading.

"You've never...?" Casey prompted.

"I-I've never come with another man before...like, in person."

I hissed through my teeth.

What a sad excuse for a man—for a person in general —to not prioritize their partner's pleasure.

Shaking my head, I forced a chuckle. I wanted her to cross that finish line more than ever. "No God here, baby girl. But that's okay. Who needs God when you have two Navy SEALs ready to become your God, right? Two men who are willing to become your Daddy? Two men in love, who want you to come so bad before they rewire your brain entirely. Right, love?"

"Right. Fuck, I bet the word *Daddy* would sound so good coming from her lips. You think you can say that for him, darlin'? He'll just want to fuck a baby into you even more."

My head snapped up to Casey.

We hadn't talked to her about that in detail just yet.

I opened my mouth, ready to backtrack for him, when Rory's moans filled the air instead. "Yes! Yes, Daddy. God, yes. Breed me whenever you want. Make me hump your leg like this. Make me earn your cum. Make me earn your baby. Fuck!"

Oh, I was definitely leaking into my boxers and uniform.

Fuck me.

My control snapped as I growled, "Come then. Hump my leg like the desperate little girl you are, and come for your Daddies. Come for your masked military men. If you want it so bad, fucking show us how you come apart."

Like a ticking time bomb, I watched as she approached the cliff—using *me* to get off.

It was the hottest sight of my fucking life.

Casey spoke next. "We'll both breed that little cunt, too. You'll take both of us. Someday, at the exact same time. You'll be crying out for your Daddies, for God, and for whoever else you think will give a fuck, all while you cream on us. This is just the beginning, darlin'. Do you really think we'll let you go after this?"

"Fuck, fuck, fuck, fuck," she babbled.

She was *right* there.

But our girl needed something more.

Something that someone else took from her.

Quickly, I took Casey's knife out of his free hand, and held it to her soft, delicate throat. It scratched at her skin as she thrashed against us. Her eyes snapped back up to me as her breathing escalated to an almost scary rate. My words were deadly. "Come on my fucking leg, you little slut. Come for Daddy. Come like you would have if the man who hurt you actually gave a fuck about you like we do. Fucking. Come."

Just like that, we both watched as her eyes rolled into the back of her head. Her back arched out, moans guttural, as her pussy spasmed underneath all of her clothing. I could feel its heartbeat on my leg. One of her hands gripped Casey's thigh as the other gripped my vest, using us both as she rubbed out the height of her orgasm on me.

Seconds passed like that. None of us moved. Casey and I were wound as tight as she was right before she orgasmed.

Eventually, her breathing slowed slightly, and her head dropped down on my chest. I raked my fingers through her silky hair in comforting way. Though, it was mere seconds later when her shoulders began shaking, and concern lit me aflame.

Casey rubbed her back gently. "Rory, sweetheart. Tell us your safe word."

She sniffled but spoke with no hesitation. "Flower."

I asked, "Do you need to stop? We can end the night right here. Get you cleaned up and put to bed."

Surprisingly, she shook her head before looking up at us. The tears on her face made her blue eyes shine like diamonds, and it was as beautiful as it was heartbreaking. "No. I need more. Please. Make me forget him. That was...so good. I need more of whatever that was. And what you said at the end—I loved it. I need more. These are good tears. I promise. I'm just feeling a lot of things right now, and it's weird."

I looked at Casey right as he looked at me. At that point in our relationship, we probably had a form of telepathic communication without even knowing.

He didn't hesitate.

His knife was against our doe's precious throat. My eyebrows raised underneath my mask as I noticed the sharp part of the blade was actually angled at her flesh. Granted, I knew Casey wouldn't kill her—even accidentally. We were trained to know exactly how to wield weapons. It was simply the choice itself.

Seems like my little boy had a knack for blood, after all.

Rory's eyes went wide as she spoke. "Wh-what are you doing?"

Lowering my knee from the apex of her thighs, I tugged at her hair and chuckled  mockingly. The action pressed her closer to Casey's knife, and I could have sworn I felt my cock twitch as I watched the pinprick of blood that began beading on her skin. "We gave you a chance to stop."

Casey singsonged back, "And you didn't."

I smirked. "You know what happens to sweet little prey who say they can handle themselves?"

Rory swallowed, and I bit back my groan as I watched the action force the blade into her skin just a little more. She didn't even wince. "What?"

My voice was as dark as the night around us, and I took immense pleasure as I watched her face grow redder from the intensity that surrounded her. "They get chased. They get put in their place. And then they get *fucked*."

My eyes moved to Casey as he lowered the knife and stepped around her. Without another word, he raised his mask, grabbed the front of my uniform with one hand and raised my mask with the other, and smashed his mouth to mine. I didn't hesitate to kiss him back. A groan reverberated out of my throat at the feel of him on me, knowing she was watching.

It was over seconds later, and I smirked at him as he pulled away—nipping at his bottom lip possessively.

We turned both of our gazes back to the woman I

already knew we would marry one day as we put our masks back in place. "Run, little doe. We'll give you a head start."

She blanched. "Both of you?"

I leaned forward, resting my hands on my knees and turning my head to the side. The gesture was nothing short of humiliating—as though I was talking to a child who was too innocent to understand demands. But the smile hidden behind my night vision gear was wolfish. "Both of us. Now. Fucking. *Run.*"

MY STOMACH TIGHTENED itself into a knot as I stared at the men in front of me. Aiden stayed crouched down in front of me, and a blush stained my cheeks at the realization that he was mocking me—yet, the ache between my thighs only intensified.

I moved my gaze to Casey next. He only stared down at me. Just like that, the absolute golden retriever of a man in front of me turned into the trained hunter that he was.

My hand went up to wrap around my throat. When I pulled it away and noticed the blood on my shaking hands—the conclusion struck me full-force: I was nothing but prey to them at that moment.

Just like I wanted.

Just like *I* requested.

The realization was the only thing I needed before I

was twisting away and sprinting in the opposite direction. My sneakers propelled me forward, and I whimpered as the branches swiped at my legs and ankles in vicious lashes. I knew without a doubt in my mind they were beyond scratched up, but I pushed forward regardless.

*Not the first time you've done this*, my subconscious whispered. It'll just be the best time.

My breath came out in heavy pants as I ran deeper into the forest. I pushed myself harder than I ever had, forcing my legs to carry me as far as they possibly could.

But the farther I ran, the less light I had.

Pausing behind a tree after minutes of running, I tried to control my breathing as I lifted my hand in front of my face.

I could hardly see myself.

But they had night vision goggles.

*Unfair.*

For the briefest of moments, I hoped to God that I wasn't actually going to get murdered in the woods.

But...at least they gave me an orgasm first, if that were the case.

Almost as if they had heard my thoughts, the distinct sound of leaves crunching grew closer before a solid *thud* echoed against a tree directly in front of me. My head snapped up at the sound, and I swallowed roughly as I saw Casey's knife embedded into the tree. The same knife that had cut me just minutes ago. A dark laugh, far too close for comfort, rang out immediately after. "Oh, c'mon now, darlin'. We know you can do better than that. We may be some old, geriatric men...but this is just insulting."

My eyes widened.

How the fuck...?

Aiden's voice came next. They both sounded like they were directly behind me. "Keep going. I know you ran harder than this for him. Fucking go!"

My heart sank for the briefest of moments.

But then adrenaline kicked in full force.

Just like they wanted.

I pushed my body away from the tree behind me and sprinted from the sound of their voices. Leaves and twigs crunched beneath the weight of my stride, and my breathing came out in rushed, heavy pants. I felt my hair yank on branches as I flew beneath them, and I winced as one particular tree branch swiped directly at the cut on my abdomen from earlier.

As I kept running, my eyes widened at the sight of lights emerging from the tree line.

Lights from the neighboring beachside hotels that John constantly talked shit about.

I stopped short at the realization and ducked behind another tree.

Fuck. Fuckity, fuck, fuck.

If I kept running, I'd be in clear lighting. Not only would they find me, but the likelihood of some poor, random tourist finding me would be even higher.

My head shook immediately. *Fuck no.* It wasn't even an option to consider.

I turned my gaze behind me and swallowed roughly.

My only option was to turn around.

I didn't give myself a second to overthink it.

Forcing a deep breath into my lungs, I swiveled once again and ran right back in the direction I came from. My legs and lungs ached, and I realized then and there that I would *absolutely* be going back to the gym if I wasn't murdered by the end of the night.

My skin itched as I pushed myself forward even more. I didn't know if I had much more strength to continue. I had to have run over three miles by that point, and exhaustion was quickly settling in.

Trent's voice filled my head as I ran.

*"What a little whore you are. I wonder if you spread your legs in town when I'm not around. Is that why you don't want me anymore?"*

Tears lined my vision.

*"My pathetic excuse for a wife."*

The sound of a gun clicking.

*"I should've killed you when you killed our baby."*

I stumbled on a stump, and my thoughts were cut short as I slammed into the ground below me with an *oomph*. I crumbled to the forest floor as all the air was knocked out of my lungs. A breath wheezed out of me, and I gripped a handful of leaves in an attempt to get my bearings.

My body shook as more adrenaline than ever before filled me.

Seconds later, when I had begun to feel a semblance of air returning to my airways—a laugh sounded from above me, stealing it away once again. The sound of a click filled the air before the beam of a flashlight bathed my form.

My eyes traveled up, squinting against the harsh light.

Casey spoke first. "Found you."

A NEED unlike any other filled me as I stared down at our little doe panting heavily. Sweat beaded at her hairline and on her arms as if she had run a marathon. She was a mess. Small cuts covered her entire body, and I knew without a doubt in my mind that she would also be covered in bruises by tomorrow morning.

My dick strained against the buttons of my uniform.

I'd tend to them later, I decided.

I needed her wrapped around me *now*.

Aiden spoke, forcing me out of my haze. "You did good, pretty girl."

While her eyes looked tortured at first—the praise seemed to melt her, and I watched as she relaxed underneath our gazes for the briefest of seconds.

The sight undid me once and for all.

Then I was on her.

Tossing the flashlight to Aiden—not caring if he

caught it at all—I ripped the mask off my face and threw it behind me. Rory gasped as she watched me come down on her fully, eyes widening as my frame covered hers without hesitation. I molded my mouth to hers, while furiously tugging at her hair and straining her neck at the angle I wanted her. My tongue slipped into her mouth seconds later, and I groaned as it stroked against hers.

The action felt like electricity zipping down my spine.

Fuck me.

I shifted us, rolling around in the dirt and leaves so I laid against the forest. Like the good girl she was, she kept her mouth on mine the entire time, moaning softly.

With one last stroke of my tongue, I pulled away breathless. "I need to fuck you, darlin'."

She smiled down at me with the sexiest grin. "So fuck me then."

I didn't waste a single second.

Moving my hands away from her waist, I pulled my dick free. I hissed at the feel of my own hand against myself, and I only prayed that I would be able to last once I was seated inside of her.

Aiden spoke, dragging our attention to him. I smirked as I saw him leaned back against the tree, arms crossed. Nothing but pure dominance and cockiness adorned his features. "Stand up, Rory. Shorts off."

She did exactly what she was told without hesitation. Biting her lip, she stood shakily and undid her shorts. They fell at her feet and she kicked them off haphazardly before turning back to Aiden.

His gaze was directly on her ass, and I had to bite back my chuckle. Always such an ass man. "You know what to do, pretty girl."

In the low lightning, I couldn't see her complexion—but I just knew she was blushing.

She lowered herself back down, and I groaned as I felt her wetness against my thigh. "C'mere, baby. Let me fill that tight little cunt. You want it?"

She nodded. "I want it."

"Ride me."

She snorted. "Ran miles through the woods and now I have to ride you, too? Gosh. A girl has to do everything around here."

Aiden barked out a laugh. "Yeah, well...someone is *very* particular on not giving you a potential UTI. He says it's very important."

Rory wiggled closer to me, and I groaned as I watched her hover right above my cock. I could feel precum building at my tip, and I ached to fill her as deeply as I possibly could. She turned back toward Aiden. "Do you guys not have doctors on base? I have health insurance."

I could feel Aiden's gaze on me in his signature *told you so* look.

I rolled my eyes.

And then my eyes rolled for an entirely different reason as Rory began to sink down on my length. A whimper tore out of my throat as I reached up and grabbed her by the waist. She squirmed against my hold, and the action only forced her to sink down more.

"Fuuuuuuck," I groaned.

"You're so big," she panted. "So fucking thick. Am I sitting on a water bottle? Holy shit."

I laughed.

And then I shifted my hips up, forcing her to take the rest of me.

She screamed out, collapsing forward. I felt her pussy spasming as she took me down, already tightening as if she were close, and my eyes rolled back at the feeling of it.

"Are you on birth control?" I hissed out.

She whimpered and pulled herself up slightly. "No."

I grabbed her waist again and angled my legs so they were bent at the knees. Pressing my heels into the dirt beneath me, I grunted. "Good. Because I'm about to pump you full of my fucking babies."

One of her hands slammed down on my sternum as I thrust into her, moaning.

She was wrong about one thing.

She wasn't going to ride me.

The one thing about being a bottom in a queer relationship for many years?

Topping from the bottom was a fucking skill I had mastered.

My breath came out jagged as I continued thrusting into her wet heat. "Yeah? You want that, little girl? You want us to come in you? Want us to breed you? Fill that pussy with so much cum that there's no question of being pregnant?"

"Ye-ye-yeesss," she moaned out.

I could already feel my balls tightening as I fucked her, and the feeling only intensified as she slammed down on me, meeting my thrusts. My eyes cut to Aiden as he stepped forward. I only thrust into her harder and faster as he spoke, "How about you come on his dick first, yeah? Milk that cum out of him. Earn it, little girl."

She nodded deliriously before slamming herself down on me.

We were both right there.

Aiden dropped to his knees before us, only to wrap one hand around her throat while the other hand wrapped around mine.

I hissed. "Fuck, Wolfe. I'm not gonna fucking last. She feels too good."

He laughed but directed his attention to her. Her eyes were locked on mine, even as Aiden squeezed at the sides of her throat hard. "Come for your Daddies, pretty girl. We're both Daddy to you from here on out. And you're going to make us a daddy for real one day, so take that cum deep in your pussy so we can breed that womb."

His deep voice rocked us both.

With his fingers tightening on the sides of my throat next, my eyes rolled into the back of my head as heat pulled at the base of my spine and abdomen. Rory gasped and moaned, rocking back and forth as she chased her own pleasure, and it was mere seconds before her walls viscously clamped down on me.

I gripped her waist harder than ever as my orgasm hit —likely leaving bruises in their wake.

I didn't give a single fuck.

"Fuck, yes." The growl was guttural as it left my lips.

"Take my fucking cum in that womb. Milk me, darlin'. Milk it all fucking out. Oh, fuck!"

Aiden moaned as he watched us fall apart under him.

It only made it better.

"Yes, yes, yes!" Rory screamed out. "Fuck, Daddy!"

Wave upon wave of pleasure rolled through us both as our orgasms mixed. Eventually, our movements became jerky and slowed until we stopped altogether.

The sound of Rory's tinkling laugh filled the space. "Oh...my God."

Aiden slowly released both of our throats. "Nah. No God here. Just your Daddies."

I groaned as Rory's pussy clenched down on my length again.

And then I smiled.

The rest of our lives were going to be so much fun.

## RORY

THE DRIVE to their house was less than five minutes, and I couldn't help but laugh at the irony of everything. My shoulders shook as I tried to swallow my laughter down in the passenger seat—Casey opting for the back so I could have more of the heat ventilation—as Aiden turned into their driveway.

Aiden looked to me with a sideways glance. They had both taken off their masks once we made it to the car, and I was finding it hard not to drool at either of their complexions. "What's so funny, pretty girl?"

"Erm." I chuckled. "I joined a kink app that allows for anonymous members anywhere in the world, found not one, but *two* men within twenty-four hours of downloading it, and they happen to live less than ten minutes away from me. Not to mention I am still getting over the fact that I just came on your knee and your boyfriend, so..."

Casey popped his head in between us. I blushed brightly as he pressed a quick kiss to my cheek, and then to Aiden's. His words followed him as he hopped out of the car. "Sounds like fate to me. Welcome home, darlin'."

It was Aiden's turn to laugh. He shook his head as he turned off the ignition, got out of the car, and walked around to open my door. "Oh, it's something alright. C'mon. You need warmer clothes. Or a hot shower. Or no clothes and body heat. All of the above could work, actually."

I stared up at him in confusion as he looked down at me expectantly. "Did you just open my door for me?"

He squinted. "...Yes?"

"Why?"

"Why not?"

I blinked. "Because I can do it myself?"

"That's fantastic news. I'm glad to hear your motor skills are still working after multiple spine-tingling orgasms. Is that supposed to be revolutionary to me, though?" He snorted before reaching over me, unbuckling my seatbelt, and scooping me into his arms bridal-style, like I weighed absolutely nothing to him.

Then he was carrying me into his home like it was the most casual thing in the world. My mind reeled at the simplicity of it. "Is this normal? Guys doing this?"

His head tilted back and forth as he weighed his next set of words "Normal? Probably not. We live in a societal time where people don't actually respect their partners like they claim. But it is normal *to me*, and something you should expect and get used to very quickly. I pamper those who are mine."

My heart rate immediately sped up. "And I'm yours now? Just like that?"

I jumped as Casey's voice sounded from down the hallway, right as he exited a room in nothing but gray sweatpants. "You could be."

My eyes raked down the lines of muscle that covered Casey, and my mouth went dry—both from the sight of the extremely muscular man and his confidently spoken words. "O-okay."

I wanted to facepalm.

Answer of the fucking year when the discussion of being owned by two strangers came into the equation.

My therapist was going to request a lobotomy for the both of us with that one.

It was as overwhelming as it was exciting, though. Because while I had known that this was what they wanted—a third to add to their dynamic and family as a whole—it was still a much different experience to hear it spoken aloud.

Anyone could give someone empty promises through a text.

But I was coming to the conclusion that Aiden and Casey meant everything they said.

"I need to get out of this uniform," Aiden said as he slowly lowered me to my feet, breaking me out of my thoughts as he walked in Casey's direction. "*Someone* obviously beat me to it and forgot his manners."

"Whaaaat," Casey groaned in mock offense, only to wink at me. "I was more than happy to put on our gear for the darling girl, but we wear that shit way too much. It was time for the sweats. And I kissed you both, so my duties as the designated golden retriever were complete."

I giggled and teased back, pushing any and all of my thoughts to the side. "Listen, I'm team sweatpants if it means I get to drool at both of your arms and abs. I am just a girl at the end of the day, ya know."

"Mmm," Casey purred as he stalked toward me. He had definitely sprayed some sort of cologne on himself since changing, and the smell of spicy woods nearly made me drool. "You can touch us, if you want. I've heard that hands-on experience is much better than the surveillance."

My blush was intense and instantaneous.

It feels so unnatural to be so horny and flirty when I'm generally so shy.

Talking to them was much easier over text.

He continued teasing me. "No? So very shy now. I could always make you, if you'd prefer that. I bet you'd be a good girl on your knees for us."

I took a deep breath right as Aiden appeared next to Casey again in matching gray sweatpants with two glasses of amber liquid in his hand. He handed one of the glasses to Casey, and the blush on my face grew as my eyes raked over both of them.

Muscles.

Tattoos.

Stance.

The words they were saying.

The *very* visible shape of their lengths in their sweatpants.

I felt like I was about to be eaten alive by two wolves as they stared back at me. With my shorts still damp from my arousal, my shirt still split in two from Casey's knife, and the hunger in their eyes...

Frankly...I wanted it.

My legs shifted as my clit pulsed with need at their attention.

What has my life become?

Aiden smirked down at me. "Everything okay, pretty girl? Do you want to sit down?"

I shook my head as I forced the words out of my mouth. "What's that you're drinking?"

Casey responded for him. "Whiskey. Would you like some?"

"I've never had it before."

Aiden smirked, almost as if a lightbulb had gone off in his head. I swallowed roughly. "You hear that, Wraithe? She's never had any whiskey before."

It was almost as if they had their own secret language as their smirks and stances began to match the other's. Casey shook his head and walked toward me slowly. "I think we should give her a taste, yeah?"

I swallowed roughly and reached for the glass.

I probably needed the drink, anyway.

"*Tsk, tsk, tsk*. Not like that," Casey corrected before taking a swig of the liquid in his glass. I watched in complete and utter confusion, my neck craning up toward him as he drew even closer to me. As quick as lightning, I gasped when one firm hand wrapped around my throat and squeezed gently. He tugged me even closer to him, our bodies flush, before he leaned down and promptly spit the liquid into my mouth.

Oh my God.

My eyes stayed wide open and locked on his as the burning liquid filled my mouth. It was an odd mix of smoke, heat, cinnamon, and caramel, yet bold enough to make my face pinch the slightest bit. A part of me wanted to cough and reject the liquid, but the other part of me craved so much more.

Casey's eyes grew heavy as he took in my reaction. "What do you think, darlin'?"

I swallowed it down. "It's...good."

"Yeah? You want some more?"

Almost as if I were in a trance, I nodded my head. He smiled brightly before angling his face back and taking another swig of the alcohol. His other hand squeezed at my throat firmer this time as he directed me to him. My mouth opened for him wide, and just like before, we both watched as the whiskey poured directly from his mouth and into mine.

It was the hottest thing anyone had ever done to me.

I closed my mouth this time and let the flavor of the alcohol fully sit on my tongue before I swallowed. His hand relinquished its grip from my throat, only to move up to my mouth. Using the pad of his thumb, he pulled my bottom lip down, stuck his thumb in my mouth, and pressed down on my tongue. Exactly as Aiden had done earlier that night.

I sucked on it eagerly as though it was chaser.

He groaned. "Good fucking girl."

Seconds later, I watched as he gulped down the rest

of the whiskey for himself, slammed the glass on the table with his own rough swallow, and slammed his mouth against mine. Our mouths and tongues moved in a tandem dance—both tasting exactly like their drink of choice. I moaned against him, unable to help the way my hips immediately shifted closer to him, too.

I needed him.

I needed both of them.

Like clockwork, Casey drew back and looked over his shoulder to Aiden, who had propped himself against the doorway to enjoy the show. "Your turn, love."

My mouth dropped and my head began to spin.

I was going to be utterly pissed if this was all a dream.

Though, as Aiden approached us and my heart began to speed into unhealthy levels, I knew better.

The heart attack I was feeling would have woken me up.

Quickly, Casey grabbed me before walking us backward. I was a puppet on strings to his strength, but for once in my life, I didn't find it difficult to surrender myself to another. After a few steps, he stopped, and I could tell that his back was against the wall as my back was yet again flush against his chest.

No knife that time.

No masks.

No outside elements to scratch at us.

No danger, outside of the men themselves.

And yet, I still felt like prey.

Their prey.

It was addicting.

Aiden towered over us, just like he had in the forest. "You think you can handle some more?"

My answer was immediate. "Yes, please."

I meant what I told them.

They may have been more strangers than not, but they had already been more considerate than anyone in my life. And it made me need them more than ever.

Plus, I had their legal names if I needed it for any reason.

Aiden smiled before following in Casey's actions. He took a sip from the glass in his hand—a matching set to Casey's—and swished it in his mouth as though it were mouthwash. When I went to open my mouth, I was cut short as his hand shot up to grip my jaw tightly. He pinched my face, forcing my mouth to open, and spit the liquid directly down my throat.

That time, I coughed as it went directly down my throat, burning and stinging everything in its wake.

As the coughs subsided, Aiden released his hold on my face. "You got your tasting with Wraithe. But I want you to feel nice and loose for what we're about to do to you. That one was just to get you tipsy faster."

My eyes flit back and forth between them. "What are you going to do to me?"

Casey responded as one of his large, strong hands moved from my waist to unbutton my shorts. I gasped as his fingers expertly pressed into the sensitive parts of my flesh. "We're going to make you feel so good, baby."

Aiden smirked. "Maybe make you beg for it a little bit, though."

"Easy there, Wolfe. Let's not overwhelm the baby just yet."

Aiden huffed petulantly before leaning down and pressing his lips to mine. His touch was firmer than Casey's, and yet, I couldn't help how my body bent to him. It was almost like a part of me needed his firmness, along with Casey's gentleness.

They were my definition of hot and cold.

Warmer and colder.

My hips shifted forward as Casey continued exploring me, all while Aiden devoured my mouth. I knew without a doubt in my mind that I was soaking Casey's fingers. And he hadn't even actually fucked me with them yet.

I was aching to be filled. Again.

My head swam between my need for them and the alcohol beginning to hit my bloodstream.

"I need this. Please. Please, fuck me."

Casey groaned, and I moaned directly along with him as he slowly inserted two fingers into me. The pressure from them alone, paired with the sensitivity of my orgasm from earlier, was enough to make my back arch. "Alright, maybe I'm wrong. She sounds so pretty when she begs."

"She does, doesn't she?" Aiden remarked as his mouth began peppering kisses along my jaw and neck. Casey only moved his fingers inside me faster.

"Oh my God," I moaned. "I'll beg. I'll do whatever you want. I just need this. Please."

My back arched even more as Casey added his thumb to my clit.

Fuck, I was going to come already.

Casey chuckled. I turned my head up to look at him as his assault on my pussy never ceased. "I feel that pretty little cunt fluttering against me. You gonna come for us already, darlin'? We haven't even gotten your shorts off yet, and we're gonna make you come a second time. This is how real men take care of their woman. Understand?"

"Oh my God, oh my God, oh my God," I moaned. I felt a bead of sweat building at my hairline between his words and their body heat. "Pleaseeeee. Dadddyyy."

Aiden spoke next. "Come on my boyfriend's fingers. Remind him how tight that pussy can get."

My eyes rolled as he finger-fucked me harder than ever.

Yet again, I had never felt so good in my fucking life.

My legs shook as I neared the edge of the cliff.

Aiden's voice sounded again, right as he shifted his head to pinch my face and look directly into my eyes. "Come for Daddy, pretty girl. Then I'll fuck that baby into you. You want it? You can have it. Right here, right now. I'll pump my cum right into your sexy body. All while Casey holds you open for me. I need you to come again first, though."

Like clockwork, my legs went to close against Casey's hand as my climax slammed into me, only to be met with resistance as Aiden's hands forced them to remain open.

I was the subject of both of their brutal assaults as a scream tore out of my throat. "Fuck! Fuck. Fuck, Daddy. I'm coming on his hand. Oh my God, fuck!"

Aiden growled. "Good fucking girl. Come on his hand. You can come on my cock next. Such a good girl."

It felt like the orgasm would last forever.

My ears rang and my body went slack against Casey as the high subsided moments later. Casey leaned down to rest his cheek against my head. "Good girl. Hottest shit of my life."

A delirious laugh left me. "You're telling me."

Aiden wasted no time.

With Casey's fingers still inside of me, Aiden dropped to his knees and tugged my shorts off. I watched with rapt attention as he took Casey's fingers out of me, locked eyes with me, and sucked my cum off of them.

Casey moaned as we watched.

Aiden stood seconds later. "I'm going to devour that pussy soon. We both are. But I need to cum first. C'mere."

And without hesitation, just like Aiden had said moments before, Casey hoisted me up like a doll, my head now directly next to his on the wall, and spread my legs for Aiden.

# TWELVE

## RORY

"FUCK," Aiden groaned out. "Your pussy is so fucking pretty."

Casey joined in on the praise. "I know I haven't seen it in full lighting just yet, but believe me, darlin'—I'm in full agreement with him. You really are a good girl with such a pretty pussy."

I whimpered. Their words were lighting me on fire. "Please. I need you. I need *something*."

"Oh?" Aiden asked as he slowly lowered his sweatpants. I watched hungrily as his cock bobbed out, hard and thick. I bit my lip to contain the moan that wanted to slip out from the sight of him wrapping his hand around it like he had done my neck earlier. "Is this what you need?"

He was big.

Easily bigger than anyone I had sex with before.

No wonder he was so arrogant sometimes. He could be with a cock that big.

I nodded my head like a needy whore, then yelped when I felt Casey bite my shoulder. My eyes swiveled to him as he soothed the bite with a lick. "Use your words, darlin'."

I huffed. "Yes, that's what I need, Daddy. Please!"

"Yeah? Tell me what you need exactly then."

If I weren't being held up—literally, suspended in the air—by a fucking giant military man, I would have huffed and petulantly stomped my foot. I swallowed roughly and forced the filthy words out of my mouth. "I need you to fuck me with your dick while my other Daddy holds me up for you."

My eyes tracked Aiden's movement as he fisted his length slowly—appreciatively, as he stared at us both. I knew without even having to look that Casey was as captivated by the man in front of us as I was. And without another word—consumed by the need that had all three of us in a chokehold—Aiden dragged his cock up and down my slit, spreading my wetness along his length.

"Touch Casey's dick over his sweatpants," Aiden muttered before slamming into me.

"Fuck!" I screamed before doing exactly what he ordered. My left hand flew down and gripped Casey's hard length over his sweatpants, squeezing and shifting along with Aiden's thrusts as he languidly pumped into me. Casey moaned and shifted to rest more of our weight against the wall. "Ohhhh my God. You're so big. How are you bigger than Casey? I didn't even think you'd fit. Holy shit."

Casey moaned. "Why do you think we needed you to come a couple times first, eh?"

Aiden's next thrust was sharp, making my eyes roll back. "Just wait until the day we fit both of our cocks into this tight little hole. We're going to make you come until you're pushing us away, and then we're going to tie you up and keep going."

My mouth dropped open in pleasure, and I began moving my hand over Casey in tandem with Aiden's thrusts. "You'd do that?"

"Oh, Rory," Casey huffed out. "You're killing me here. Of course we would."

Aiden laughed before leaning down to kiss Casey. His thrusts never ceased as he continued to pound into me. Unable to help myself, I used my other hand to rub my clit in short circles as I watched them enjoy each other —even as he continued to abuse me in the most delicious way.

Aiden pulled away from him, eyes hazy, before turning to me and slanting his mouth directly on mine. And like before, I immediately granted him access and allowed him to invade my mouth. Our tongues tangled, moans mixing, as the three of us lost each other to the sea of pleasure that invaded us.

And we welcomed it.

Casey groaned. "Darlin'. Stop. You're gonna make me come in my sweats."

Aiden broke our kiss and laughed. He pumped even

harder into me as he spoke to me directly. "Don't you dare stop stroking him."

"Oh my God," Casey moaned. "You're such a fucking asshole."

Aiden winked in his direction. "You've brought up coming in your uniform, jeans, and sweats so many times over the last couple of weeks. Time to fucking do it."

My words were broken up with Aiden's thrusts. "Is-is that not e-embarrassing?"

Aiden rested his forehead against mine. "So? He'll be a good boy and embarrass himself for me then. Won't you, love?"

His answer was immediate. "Yes, Daddy."

"Atta boy. Embarrass yourself in front of our girl. You come in your sweatpants, and I'll pump that baby we both want into her. Got it?"

"Yes, Daddy. Oh my God. Rory, stroke me. I want him to come inside you so fucking bad. Stroke me like you wish he was fucking you."

Aiden's eyes flew down to my hand as I did exactly what he said. And as I squeezed Casey, pumping him in hard, firm strokes, Aiden matched the exact tempo.

He was fucking us both through me.

My back arched off Casey as I felt Aiden hit a spot deep inside me that had my toes curling. "Daddy! Fuck!"

That seemed to undo Casey. "Oh my God. Yes. Yeah, he's our Daddy. Fuck, I'm coming. Oh my fucking God, Rory, don't stop. Holy shit!"

Aiden kept stroking and hitting that spot as he growled out, "Give it to me. Both of you."

He didn't even need to do or say anything else.

Between Casey's moans, my G-spot being hit for the first time ever, and the simple presence of them both—I all but screamed as yet another orgasm hit me like a tsunami. It wasn't the typical climax of waves of pleasure, but rather one gigantic wave that obliterated you and everything you knew. My toes curled as they hung in the air, calves flexing, my hands digging into anything they could. In which case, it happened to be Casey's dick and Aiden's arm.

My ruiners were my life vest at the same time.

As we fell off our cliffs, Aiden moaned roughly at my pussy tightening around him, and seconds later, he was forcing his entire length inside of me—pressing and coming right against my cervix. He growled like a man possessed, and I cried out as I felt his cock jerk and pulse inside of me. "Take. My. Fucking. Cum. Both of our babies are gonna be in that tight cunt tonight."

I cried out again at his words.

They were far, far too hot.

As Aiden slowed his movements, I turned my head up to look at Casey.

He was already staring at me with a look akin to wonder etched in his features.

Ever so slowly, after a few moments had passed, Aiden took himself out of me and helped Casey slowly lower me to the floor. My balance was unsteady, and I blushed furiously under both of their gazes.

And then...I reached in between my legs and smeared some of the mess on my fingers.

Aiden's eyebrows pinched together as he watched me.

I smirked at him before using my other hand to crook a finger at him. His eyebrows furrowed, but he did as I requested, bending down. I dragged him closer—all of us within an inch of one another—before placing my cum-covered fingers in his mouth.

Casey made a sound of disbelief as he watched Aiden surrender to me, sucking his own cum off of my fingers languidly. "Holy shit."

Aiden's eyes snapped open, landing on mine, before moving to Casey.

Slowly, he pulled away from my hand as we all stood there, panting, with a gentle smile on his face. "Topping from the bottom, huh, pretty girl? That's a dangerous game. We can play it with you, though."

I smiled along with him. "Casey isn't the only one who can do it."

He lifted his head and raised an eyebrow at him. "Oh, really?"

Casey changed topics immediately. "Okay, well...I just came in my pants. Can we go shower now?"

The laugh that escaped me was nothing short of genuine.

Aiden shook his head, but there was no erasing the sated smile on his face. "C'mon. Both of you. We all need one after that."

Casey laughed. "And a fucking nap."

STEAM WAFTED throughout the gigantic bathroom as Aiden and Casey gingerly peeled me out of my soiled, cut-up T-shirt and bra. They were already naked themselves, quickly shedding their sweatpants. My eyes roamed over them appreciatively.

I didn't know for a fact where we were going to end up.

We could have all decided this would be a simple one-night-stand and move on with our lives.

And because of that thought, I allowed myself free reign to appreciate the scary, yet gentle, men before me. The men who could kill someone in a heartbeat, and yet continued to treat me as though I was the most delicate flower to exist.

I loved it.

Aiden leaned down and kissed my shoulder affection-ately. "Are you okay?"

I nodded my head without a second's hesitation. "I'm good."

And for once, it wasn't a lie.

I was good.

Casey kissed my other shoulder before leaning down and digging through their bathroom vanity. Seconds later, he stood tall with a green first-aid kit in his hands. I watched as he laid it down on the vanity, opened it up, and reached for the peroxide and waterproof bandages. He dropped down to his knees and inspected the cut on my abdomen from earlier as Aiden walked behind me and wrapped his arms around my chest sweetly. He rested his chin against my shoulder, and I leaned back to enjoy his warmth.

Casey's face pinched as he drizzled the peroxide on the cut, forcing a whimper out of me. It was the same effect as he tended to the cut on my throat and the multiple scrapes along my legs. "I'm sorry, darlin'. Need to make sure you're good."

"It's okay." I smiled down at him, trying to hide my wince. "Comes with the territory, right?"

He placed a kiss on my stomach in response. Butter-flies filled me at the action. "They won't scar. I didn't think they would, but just so you know."

I snorted. "Wouldn't be the first scar I've gotten."

Aiden's arms tightened around me instantly, and Casey's eyes shot up to me. While I held humor in my tone, they held...anger. "Is that son of a bitch dead?"

I immediately sobered. "Yes."

Aiden relaxed against me as Casey nodded. "Good. He would have been within the week if he wasn't."

I blinked. "You shouldn't say things like that. You guys don't know me."

Aiden spoke directly in my ear, and I shivered as his warm breath spread against my flesh. "We don't have to know someone inside and out to know that they don't deserve to be treated like dog shit. But even still—you're already special to us. So, yes. I agree with him."

A sense of wonder flit through me at their words.

Had I really been the subject of the worst kind of love, all while men like this existed?

Casey stood again and placed a quick kiss on both mine and Aiden's mouths. No other words needed to be spoken. And as Aiden nudged me through the opened glass doors of the shower, making both of their intentions clear, the wonder in my mind simply shifted to peace.

"TELL US ABOUT HIM?" AIDEN ASKED AS WE ALL laid in their bed. The shower was quick, all of us opting to just wash the sweat and dirt away from our bodies. My hair lay damp against his chest while Casey laid on his other peck. I wore one of their T-shirts, and I could have sworn they were genuine giants once I put it on and realized it came down to my knees.

I picked my head up slightly to look at them both with a raised brow. "My husband?"

Casey hummed in response.

My head plopped back down. I know it was an innocent question, considering their reactions from earlier. And of course, they were well within their rights to ask, considering I had requested dark scenes and kinks for nothing but my own benefit.

Because of him.

"What do you want to know?"

Casey was the first to speak. "Would you have stayed if he didn't die?"

I blinked. That wasn't the question I was expecting. "I don't know. I've talked to my therapist a lot about that hypothetical since his car accident. Maybe? I didn't know any better. In fact, some days, I thought all women went through the exact same thing I did. I thought it was normal to be more of a servant than a partner. But ultimately...I was still just a girl in love with a boy who had once treated her like she was his entire world."

"Why did he stop?"

My heart squeezed in anguish at the truth. I laid out all of the words clearly. "We were pregnant. And I miscarried. He wanted to try again immediately, since the doctors said it was just an unfortunate case of ectopic pregnancy rather than anything we could have potentially done 'wrong,' but it was just so painful. I didn't want to. At one point, I didn't want to have sex at all. Then he started wearing cologne and going out more at night...and I just knew what was happening, you know? I'm not stupid."

I paused, looking over at them both, only to find both of them giving me their complete and utter attention. Casey reached for my hand and squeezed it gently.

A shudder went through me as I continued. "Then the drinking began. Then, the name calling. And it just spiraled until there was no going back. And eventually... all of my 'no's' fell on deaf ears. Except on the days that my denials turned into punishments."

Aiden's voice was heavy. "And your punishments were what we did tonight?"

I sniffled as tears lined my vision and nodded. "Yeah. Cat and mouse. He would wear scary masks, since I hated horror movies. Or initiate sex—only for it to turn into a way to gag me so I couldn't tell him to stop when it became too rough. I'm sure there are more examples, too."

Casey spoke as he squeezed my hand again. "I'm so sorry, darlin'. You didn't deserve that."

A sad laugh escaped me. "It's okay. I mean, it's not, but it is. He can't hurt me anymore. I just think I'll forever mourn that he did what he wanted to. To turn me into the victim he wanted. I crave what he forced me to go through. And I struggle with knowing if that makes me powerful or weak."

Aiden shifted. I felt his hand cup my jaw, and my eyes flew up to meet his. "I promise you, pretty girl. I have met some very weak men and women in my life. My own father was extremely abusive to me and my siblings, and that was the definition of a weak man. You are the polar opposite of that definition. And we will prove that to you every damn day for the rest of our lives if you let us."

I swallowed roughly. "I have a question."

Casey answered, "Yes?"

"What would happen if I decided I still wasn't ready

to have kids? After the excitement of tonight dies, I mean. Would you both kick me to the curb next?"

Aiden's smile was sad, but his words were firm and patient. "We wouldn't actually trap you with a child, pretty girl. Sure, we do want children. We've never lied about that. Frankly, we've been obsessed with you since we saw your first profile picture and bio on that damn app. But it is still your body and mind that will have to go through a pregnancy, and we understand that you have trauma. It is always your choice."

Casey added to Aiden's response. "We will support you no matter what."

My heart melted at the honesty they both shared.

My words were heavy. "It was hard for us to get pregnant the first time. Before the miscarriage. I don't know if it'll be easy. Or if I'll miscarry again."

Aiden pressed a kiss to my temple before laying a hand on my stomach. Casey followed his movements. "We're not here for easy."

"And if it takes time, then it takes time. We still want to try this with you," Casey added.

I smirked up at them. "For such scary, important men—you sure do have lots of big feelings."

The sound of the smack on my ass echoed throughout the room before the stinging pain even registered.

I yelped and rubbed at it with a pout. "Rude."

Aiden snorted before slapping my hand away and rubbing at the mark himself. "Brat."

Silence floated around us. Exhaustion had all of us in a tight hold, but I don't think any of us wanted to fall into the depths of sleep just yet. So I nestled into Aiden's warmth even more.

I felt safe.

I couldn't remember the last time I felt that.

Finally, I spoke the question that weighed on me the most. "What happens now?"

Casey turned to look at me. "What do you mean?"

I avoided his gaze. "Is this friends with benefits until I wind up pregnant with two baby-daddies? Do we continue talking on that app? Do we try to do...this? What happens when we wake up tomorrow and have to go back to the reality of life, jobs, and everything else?"

Aiden made a noise of understanding. "What do you want to happen?"

Casey smiled. "Yeah, darlin'. I think we've made ourselves pretty clear on what we want. But what do you want?"

I didn't even need to think about my answer.

I *knew* what I wanted.

I wouldn't have agreed to this night if I didn't want it.

I smiled at Casey before leaning over and placing a gentle kiss to his mouth, and then craned my neck up to kiss Aiden next. Both of them had their hands on me, and fire licked at my veins.

An insatiable fire that only they could cure.

I broke the kiss with Aiden as I began crawling down Aiden's body.

He sat up immediately with Casey in his wake.

My smile was downright evil. "I want to try. You both tried with me. It's only fair I return the favor, and

I've been comfortable with everything so far. But first...I want to say thank you."

Curious about Aiden's siblings? Want to see cameos of Aiden, Casey, and Rory in the future? Check out the next books in the Reckless Hearts Series if so!

Clueless: An MMF Forbidden Romance
Faceless: An MM Military Romance

Continue reading to see our beautiful throuple in this story get everything they've wished for <3

# EPILOGUE



"PLEASE TELL me you didn't lose the ring," Casey all but shouted as he tore into our closet. "Both rings? Did you actually lose *both* fucking rings?"

I leaned against the door frame, arms crossed, as I watched the love of my life throw a temper tantrum.

One of the loves of my life, I should say.

I still couldn't believe I was lucky enough to have two.

He turned to look at me, and I almost felt bad when I saw the genuine fear and worry crawling through his features.

Key word being *almost*.

"Aiden!" he barked. "What the fuck?"

I rolled my eyes before straightening and walking toward him.

We had thoroughly planned our engagement to our pretty girl.

Down to the miniscule floral décor details, in the forest that started everything.

Of course I didn't lose the fucking rings.

"Would you calm the fuck down, love?" I asked as I walked toward the bookshelf in the corner of our bedroom. It was full to the brim with romance and "romantasy" books, as Rory called them. I shook my head every time another package arrived at our door, but it made her happy, and therefore it made us equally as happy. "She was doing our laundry this morning. I didn't want her to see the boxes when putting our shirts up, so I moved them to the bookshelf since she doesn't actually read them. They're her shelf trophies, remember?"

Casey went silent. "Oh."

I laughed. "Oh? That's all?"

He sniffed. "A text message or heads up would have been nice, ya know?"

A snort left my throat at his petulant tone. "Ah, yes. Because that's so smart for a throuple who uses whatever phone is closest to them at any given point. My apologies."

"You're such a dick."

I turned to him with a smirk. "I love you, too, baby boy."

Just like that—a blush marred his skin.

I snorted. He was so easy to melt into putty.

I reached behind the highest row of books—where our darling girl couldn't even reach without a ladder— and grabbed the rings.

One from me, and one from Casey.

The one from me was simple. A basic, diamond-encrusted band. Though, to personalize it as much as possible, Casey and I had decided to engrave the day we downloaded *Preyless* into the underside of the ring.

Because if this had all failed, there was no other prey we would have wanted.

Casey's ring, however, easily stole the show.

A silver band molded into the shape of leaves, with a diamond on each side.

One diamond was clear and sharp, while the other diamond was black as coal.

Tied together through the representation of life.

It was more than fitting.

We were her diamonds, but she was our life.

I turned toward Casey and shook the box lightly. "See? We're fine. We should head to the hotel, though. She's going to be getting off soon, and we don't want to fuck this up. John can only distract her for so long. "

It was yet another trait I adored about our girl.

We had told her time and time again that she didn't have to work.

Yet, she continued to go to the hotel on the days that John was there to keep him company.

It was made even better by the fact that John actually liked us.

And so, we never protested.

Casey took a big, deep breath before nodding nervously.

It was go time.

Rory stumbled as we walked her toward the pathway of the tree line. The October air felt warmer than normal, and I couldn't have been more grateful for it. She whined, "Can you just tell me where we're going? I don't like surprises!"

Casey laughed. "We know."

"And why are you both so dressy? For a beach?"

I laughed next. "So full of questions tonight, pretty girl."

She huffed. "So lacking in answers, scary man."

Casey turned to me with a bemused smile as I shook my head.

She was lucky I was completely and utterly in love with her.

That, and I didn't want to ruin the surprise.

She would have been slung over my shoulder otherwise.

Finally, after another five minutes of walking, we made it to the exact location.

The night where everything officially started.

Fairy lights were strung amongst the trees, lit up from battery packs, with hundreds of pink flowers mixed in between and shoved throughout the foliage.

In a forest that would otherwise be dead, we had brought it to life.

Just like she had brought us to life.

I nodded to Casey as I got down on one knee, and seconds later, he untied the bandana from around her head before dropping to his knee behind her, too. We watched as she blinked against the light, only to take everything in seconds later. Her head swiveled around in confusion and awe before she turned to us.

She gasped when she saw us both down on one knee.

And then tears filled her eyes.

"Rory Vale," I started. "Two years ago, Casey and I knew that we were missing something completely and utterly vital to us. We were happy, but we were also lacking. And then, we saw you."

Casey cut in. "And to say that the last two years has been the best of our life is a complete and utter understatement. You've given us the hope and completion we needed. You've changed us, and we can only hope we've changed you, too."

I took over again. "So, would you do us the extraordinary honor of letting us call you our wife? We know we can't actually get married with the law...but we want to call you our wife, and we want you until death do us part."

She stared down at us with smeared mascara and a hand covering her mouth.

Seconds passed as the tears continued.

My stomach was beginning to sink the longer she stared at us in silence.

Right as my head began to lower, though, she dropped her hand from her face and reached into her back pocket. Casey and I turned to look at each other before she held a stick in front of us.

A pregnancy stick.

A pregnancy stick with two solid, clear lines.

Positive.

My head shot up to look her in the eyes once realization dawned on me. We were both frozen in place, absorbing the information before us.

She had told us that she was going off birth control, after going back on it for the last two years, but that was only a month ago.

Did it really happen that quickly?

Casey spoke with a shake in his voice. "Darlin'?"

Finally, she sniffled the words we both needed to hear. "I do, if you do."

# ACKNOWLEDGMENTS

To everyone in my life who has given me courage to keep living, despite going through some really tough stuff once upon a time. This list is pretty endless and I wouldn't know where to start with names if I tried. Honestly, I'm sure there are complete strangers I've only spoken to once that would fit this bill. But...I wouldn't be here without them. Genuinely. Thank you.

To Tilly, who had to listen to me bitch about this storyline for quite a while—which is hilarious given her feelings about the military and... well, men in general. That's how you know you've hit "Oh, we're good friends" level, huh?

To Sadie, who helped me form this into something magical. Thank you for everything <3

To Bria, who continues to help me grow every day, and without her, I'd be a flailing fish in the sea. Seriously. I don't know how she does it. I'm tired for her.

And lastly, to T—my best friend and bestest supporter. I wouldn't be here without you. There's so much that I could say here... but honestly, I'll just cry, and we both know that I do enough of that as-is. Just, thank you. My yellow heart, always. <3

# ABOUT

## C. S. SILVERNE

C. S. Silverne is a twenty-something year old author who spends a lot of her time hiding behind a computer as the true introvert she is—between writing words, designing pretty pictures, reading her kindle, or blaring rock/country music—it's guaranteed she's trying to ignore the world in some emo fashion.

She takes light of her pseudonym, always finding love in the silver linings of the world. Because, as we all know, sometimes—love chooses us in the strangest, cruelest of ways, and the stories of the forbidden deserved to be told.

Find C. S. Silverne at www.cssilverneauthor.com.